A New Beginning

SCOTTISH WEREBEARS BOOK 4

LORELEI MOONE

CONTENTS

PROLOGUE

As they exited the dunes and reached the beach at Applecross Bay, Matty had to smile.

His big brother, Jamie, had been right. Overnight, the sea had washed away their last attempt at building the most awesome sand castle anyone had ever seen. They'd have to start all over again.

Rather than feel discouraged, he was excited. Some of the turrets hadn't turned out quite right yesterday. Today, he would build an even better castle. And Jamie had told him to do it all by himself, so he would try extra hard.

He was only seven, but he didn't need anyone's help to build the best sand castle of the season.

Without paying too much attention to where Jamie was going, Matty got to work. Filling buckets of damp sand, and turning them over into perfectly formed shapes.

It was cloudy, a bit windy but not too cold. It was a perfect summer day.

"That's a nice castle," a voice interrupted him.

Matty looked up to find a tall man standing beside him, his hands on his hips and head cocked to the side as if he was inspecting Matty's work in great detail. Next to the man stood a woman with pale gray eyes and equally gray hair.

"Thanks. I'm not supposed to talk to strangers, though."

The man smiled at him and nodded. "That's a good rule to have."

Matty focused once more on his work, shoveling more sand into his bucket, excavating what was going to be the moat of the castle.

"Listen, Matthew," the woman spoke softly.

"You know my name?" Matty looked up again, focusing on her face this time.

"I'm Molly. You've never met me before, but I know your parents very well. They've asked me to take care of you should anything happen to them."

Matty frowned scratching his face, leaving streaks of damp sand behind on his cheek.

"Where are my parents?" he asked.

"I'm very sorry to be the one to tell you this, but..." the woman hesitated, glancing anxiously over at her male companion.

"Your parents have met with an accident. They didn't make it," the man said in a matter-of-fact tone.

Matty turned his head and looked across the empty beach, his heart racing. There was no sign of Jamie; no brotherly advice within reach.

"But I just saw mom. She was just there, at our house!" Matty protested.

"I know, darling. These things don't ever make sense," the woman said.

They really didn't. How long had he been building this castle for? It felt like he'd only just arrived at the beach.

"I don't believe you." Matty threw down his trowel and bucket and jumped up, ready to run home.

The man had other ideas and stepped up to him, grabbing him by both his arms and keeping him firmly in place. "No you don't."

"I want to go home! Let go of me!" Matty fought hard against the tears prickling in his eyes - big boys didn't cry after all, but the man's fingers tightened painfully around his arms.

"We're sorry to tell you like this. But there's nothing there for you anymore."

"Where's Jamie? Jamie!" Matty cried out.

"Jamie has gone back to the house to take care of things now that your parents are no more. But he's only a boy himself; he can't take care of you as well," the woman explained.

The man meanwhile loosened his grip on Matty's arms. "Be a good boy and don't make this any harder than it has to be. Wouldn't you want your parents to be proud of you?"

Matty nodded, biting his bottom lip. He would be a good boy. For his mom and dad.

With his head hanging low, he walked in between the two grown-ups across the beach, not up the path Jamie and he had taken earlier which led to their home, but another one that led to Applecross village.

"Wait, my bucket!" Matty suddenly remembered.

The man grabbed his arm again and shook his head. "You won't be needing that where we're going."

Matty turned one last time, seeing his red bucket and spade abandoned in the pale sand, surrounded by turrets and walls that were going to make up the best sand castle of this season, if not ever. He didn't even get to finish it.

Life *was* unfair.

The rest of the walk was silent. Matty wondered if the two adults were communicating in their thoughts like his mom and dad were able to do. Every so often, when they did say something, they seemed to disagree a lot. Probably they couldn't hear each other unless they spoke.

After the long walk through the dunes, the woman directed him into the back of a big silver car waiting in the village parking lot, while the man took a seat behind the wheel.

From the back seat, Matty looked around the village; the shops were still closed, and there was no sign of anyone around. The roads were empty as well as they drove off. There was no one to wave goodbye to. No one to notice he was leaving.

Matty didn't know where they were taking him, but he'd adjust somehow, for his parents and Jamie.

He had to be a big boy now.

CHAPTER ONE

It was an ordinary November morning in Gartcosh, a sleepy village near Glasgow. At least, Matt Argyle assumed it was, because, from the safety of his home, all mornings seemed quite similar. He had a deadline and was expecting some groceries to be delivered, but other than that, today was going to be no different than yesterday or the day before.

Matt lived alone, ever since Molly, the woman who had raised him through most of his childhood, had left this house to him. He was glad to have it, because he couldn't imagine living anywhere else. The tall fences offered some measure of privacy, but, just in case, he never stepped out of the house until after nightfall.

He hadn't left his property in years.

Just as he turned on his laptop, Matt was interrupted by an unusual sound. A mechanical hum that seemed to creep ever closer. It wasn't any of the cars his neighbors drove. No, he'd recognize those. This was something bigger.

Matt got up and peeked out the curtain. A large moving truck pulled into the road and stopped in front of the empty house next door. His heart started to beat a little faster when two men got out of the cabin and started to pile up boxes of stuff on the pavement.

It had been nice, safe, knowing that the house adjoining his backyard was unoccupied. Now it looked like that was about to change.

His anxiety grew when he started to speculate about who might be moving in there. What if it was a family with children who would inevitably drop a ball or some other toy over the fence and expect to come in and fetch it? What if the parents expected to be all sociable and get to know him?

No way, he couldn't have that.

Along with the tension of what might be, Matt felt an old feeling creep over him. This is what always happened when he least wanted it to. His skin started to itch a bit, and the muscles in his shoulders, arms, and legs seemed to throb and pulsate.

Shit, not now!

He closed his eyes and tried to will the odd sensation away. It was all in his head; he knew that. The itching, the funny feeling as if his body tried to outgrow his own skin. If he didn't get himself under control, the transformation would be complete, and he'd find himself unrecognizable.

He'd turn into a bear.

Obviously, that was impossible, but somehow his mind refused to accept the truth and continued to feed him these outlandish delusions.

It always happened when he felt threatened or under pressure.

As he opened his eyes again, he saw a modest little car pull into the road beside the truck. He held his breath for the moment of truth: the opening of the driver side door. Two shapely legs clad in denim stepped out first, then the rest of his new neighbor came into view.

She was beautiful. Her shoulder length auburn hair framed a heart-shaped face with dark, mysterious eyes that Matt couldn't bear to look at for more than a second. She was curvaceous, feminine, mesmerizing.

He only managed to catch a short glimpse before she rushed off to the backside of the truck, gesturing wildly, probably at the two men unloading her things.

This changed things. He wasn't sure how exactly, but he could feel it in his bones.

Wait a minute; he wasn't really considering meeting this woman, was he? That was simply ridiculous. He hadn't talked to any of his other neighbors in ages, not even the ones he'd known all his life.

He didn't have time for this, not today. Matt shook his head, as if to rid himself of all these strange thoughts. He had a deadline to consider, a report to write.

And anyway, it would be best for everyone involved if he stuck to his routine. What difference did it make anyway who moved in where? His house was his own; nobody could change that.

Matt sighed and forced himself away from the window. With his laptop under his arm, he retreated to the farthest part of the house, the small room at the back where he'd spent most of his childhood. It didn't have any windows, and the loud hum from the truck up front only just managed to infiltrate it.

So what if she was pretty? He was hardly relationship material.

Matt plugged his headphones into the output of the laptop and cranked up the volume, drowning out the remainder of the noise coming from outside and got to work.

———— ◆ ————

As soon as he hit 'send' on the report, many hours later, he sat back and crossed his arms. He'd finished the job, somehow, but the image of the new woman next door had never quite left him. It was maddening. How was he meant to function like this?

Just with her presence, she'd upset the entire balance of everything. He'd skipped lunch as well as dinner, something he'd never done before, simply because he didn't think he could regain focus if he accidentally spied her through the kitchen window.

He'd missed the delivery of groceries that he'd scheduled for the evening, because the music he'd been listening to had blocked out the doorbell.

Still, he couldn't stay in the back room forever. He needed to blow off steam somehow.

Scottish Werebear: A New Beginning

After preparing a quick bite, he noted with relief that there was no activity outside. Even the usual neighborhood kids playing ball in the street had gone home already, so he headed to the back of the house again and looked out at the unfinished project awaiting him.

For a few nights now, he'd been working on building a patio with a barbecue pit in the backyard. The print-out with instructions he'd found online had said it would be spacious, and the barbecue could cater to 6-8 people. Not that he was planning on using it for entertaining, but he was rather fond of grilled meat and had a very healthy appetite himself.

Of course, the new neighbor changed a few things. For one, he'd have to grow a hedge of some sort for extra privacy. Luckily, this was the right time of year to order the plants.

He didn't mind the extra work, after all, he enjoyed having things to do at night when sleep was hard to come by. Gardening had proved a welcome outlet for his energy as well as creativity. But it would cut into his area a bit, leaving less space for the seasonal vegetables he wanted to plant in spring.

But there was no point debating it. Matt picked up the instructions again and started collecting his materials. Everything he needed for the patio had already been delivered. The ground had been cleared and mostly leveled, so all he had to do was lay the stones tonight, and he'd still be right on schedule.

So he got to work. He managed to carry a dozen stones across the yard and had just begun to lay them down when something roused his suspicion. It wasn't a sound as such, more of a vibe. A presence.

He was being watched.

Just as he was trying to convince himself he was being paranoid, he turned towards his new neighbor's house and was immediately greeted by a rustle and muffled curse. She was there.

Shit, now what?

It was too dark to see properly, but that didn't deter his brain from showing him fuzzy images of her stumbling backward behind the wooden fence. Like infra-red imagery captured by a hunting scope, except he wasn't seeing them with his eyes. Of course, that wasn't possible. His brain was playing tricks on him.

Still, he couldn't take the risk, and he rushed inside. From the safety of his dark back room, he looked through the gap in the curtain while rubbing the cold out of his hands. In his eagerness to get the project done, he hadn't even realized how cold it was tonight.

Her side of the fence wasn't lit up, so there was no way of knowing for sure whether she was still there, not scientifically anyway. But now that his mind had captured her presence, he seemed to be able to track her a little.

That's impossible.

He kept scanning the fence for a few minutes until his instincts told him she'd gone.

This was too much to deal with. Even his safe haven, his personal backyard wasn't secure anymore. Something had to change.

Matt took to the one outlet still open to him. The world-wide-web. The answer ought to be out there, hopefully.

With a swiftness his fingers hadn't shown all day during his work, he typed out his experience - anonymously - aiming to publish it for the world to see on a discussion forum he often lurked in. For someone with delusions such as his, what else could he do? Where else could he go for help?

He finished his piece with questions: Was there hope? Should he try harder to ignore her? Or was this a sign that the status quo simply wasn't sustainable anymore? Perhaps he should go with it, and give in to the irrational desire to watch her, admire her, perhaps try to reach out to her even?

He didn't know right from wrong anymore. Either way, he definitely was in trouble.

And for a change, others shared in it.

In the past, he'd mostly held back, reading other people's posts instead of writing his own. He'd come to recognize some of the names of regulars who liked to comment. There was the cheerleader who supported everything and everyone, no matter how ridiculous. Next came the troll and the pessimist, each leaving their standard comments. *Go for it. Ignore her; there's no hope. Etcetera.*

The more helpful members were less prolific in their responses, but he waited for them anyway.

After an hour of waiting a few comments had come in that didn't offer much other than sympathy. Oh well, maybe later...

CHAPTER TWO

"Be careful with that, please!" Leah blurted out as she noticed the two movers unloading the truck containing her belongings a bit more enthusiastically as she would have liked.

They barely took notice and continued their work at the same pace, one all but flinging each box out of the back of the vehicle, for the other to catch and set down on the pavement.

What's the point of labeling things as fragile if they're intent on throwing them around?

Leah took a deep breath and headed for the door, clutching the key to what was going to be her new home tightly in her fist. *If anything's broken, I swear to God I'll give them an ear full and demand damages.*

Money wasn't the issue as such; Leah was most concerned about the supplies she needed to make a living from now on. Homemade candles and bath products can't just be replaced instantly by throwing money at the issue. These things take time and effort to recreate.

Her heart still hammered away in her chest as she looked around the empty hall, living area and open plan kitchen. It was a nice little bungalow, in a nice little village. Picturesque was the word. A far cry from the flat she'd called home ever since moving out on her own after her dad's death.

As she came back out, the truck was mostly unloaded, with only the larger pieces of furniture remaining inside. She bit her tongue and let the two men do their job as they saw fit, noting that despite shifting everything inside of the house at record speed, they hadn't scuffed a single wall or door frame.

The curtain-less windows facing the modest front yard

revealed that the sun was out. Odd not just for the time of year – mid-November - but also for the area. It wasn't for nothing that Scotland had the reputation of being cloudy and wet most of the year. Some stereotypes were true. But today was a perfectly bright, icy day.

Leah felt chills run down her spine and remembered that she should probably switch on the central heating. The house had sat empty for a while the rental agent had told her. Although everything looked in good condition, you could never be certain that everything would work as expected.

Luckily, everything seemed to switch on as it should, and soon she could hear the hot water stream into the large radiator below the living room window.

Leah halfheartedly told the movers where to put all her belongings, though they had pretty much done everything on auto pilot based solely on the meticulous labeling system Leah had stuck to while packing. Kitchen boxes in the kitchen and so on. *Obviously.*

Though she did do a few spot checks to make sure the contents were all intact, she couldn't find anything amiss. Soon after, the older one of the two movers presented her with a clipboard containing a form for her to sign. Then they were off, and she was left alone in her newly rented bungalow, surrounded by boxes and wrapped up furniture.

Unpacking would be a thankless task. One Leah didn't have the energy for just yet. Anyway, it wasn't like she had a job to go to come nightfall; she'd quit her night shift position at the call center a month ago.

And so the only two boxes she did open up properly were the ones containing the electric kettle and mugs, and of course, her bedding so that she could catch some rest later. Thanks to the groceries she'd picked up on her way, she soon had a steamy cup of tea in her hands as she sat down on her still wrapped up sofa.

Made it.

It was hard not to feel just a little bit nervous about the

big step Leah had taken today. She'd been ready for a change. Ready to slow down and live life somewhere quieter, on her own terms. But was this the right decision? Or the right time?

Her homemade bath supply company was just starting to pick up steam, and the internet was a fickle place to do business. What if her orders dried up suddenly? What if her savings ran out before she was able to make things work?

She took a deep breath, and then a big sip of her hot drink and tried to suppress all those doubts and worries that were attempting to claw their way to the surface.

Everything will be fine.

She closed her eyes and forced her nerves to calm, when the doorbell rang and made her spring into action yet again.

"Yes?" Leah asked, while opening the light wood front door.

"Hi!" a woman sporting a wide smile and larger than life platinum blond curls greeted her on the other side. "I'm Caroline- but everyone calls me Carrie. I noticed you moving in and thought I'd say hello and welcome you to the neighborhood!"

Leah reluctantly met the woman's outstretched hand, who warmly shook it while continuing to flash her teeth at her.

"Thank you so much. I'm Leah."

"It's nice seeing this old house in use again. It's been empty for so long..." Carrie's voice trailed off towards the end of the sentence, as if there was something she was thinking that she didn't want to share.

"It seems to be a nice area. I've been meaning to get out of the city for some time," Leah responded.

"Mhmm. It certainly is. Very good for families. Do you have children?"

Leah shook her head.

"Oh well. Maybe later, aye?"

"Right."

Carrie hadn't taken her eyes off Leah throughout the short exchange, except to inspect the as yet barren hallway behind her. She was clearly curious what this house looked like on the inside, but Leah was in no mood to invite her in. Nobody was going to come in until everything was set just how Leah wanted it.

"Anyway, I live just next door. If you ever need anything." Carrie pointed to the neatly kept house towards the right of Leah's bungalow. "I'm sure you'll meet the rest of the neighborhood shortly."

"I'm sure." Leah smiled. "So, who lives there?" Leah pointed at the other house next door to her towards the left. Its exterior was equally polished, but the windows were dark almost as if they were boarded up from the inside.

"Oh... I suppose *him* you probably won't meet. Matthew Argyle," Carrie's voice suddenly didn't seem so upbeat anymore. "He doesn't tend to mingle."

"Oh yeah? How come?" Leah tried not to sound too suspicious but was having a hard time to disguise the concern that she'd been tricked into putting down a rather sizable deposit on a house right next door to a difficult neighbor. Or worse, a pervert.

"It's not that he's not a nice guy; he's fine enough. Grew up with him. He just doesn't really socialize. Not sure what happened to him, but ever since old Mrs. Argyle passed and left him the house, he's been really withdrawn. It's a shame."

"I suppose the death of a parent can do that to a person." Although Leah was still a little suspicious, she did feel bad to have judged her new neighbor so harshly before even finding out the first thing about him. She'd had a difficult time when she'd just lost her dad years ago, so she could sympathize.

Eight years in a bad part of the city had clearly taken their toll and hardened her up. That was part of why she'd moved here, to get out of the hustle and bustle and allow herself to smell the roses more. If there was one thing she didn't want - despite herself - it was to start off on the wrong foot with her new neighbors.

"Well, thanks anyway and lovely to meet you. I'm sure we'll see each other around," Leah said her goodbyes to Carrie, who shot her one last bright smile before turning on her heel and heading back home.

Leah glanced to the left once more at the dark windows of Matthew Argyle's house before wrapping herself up tighter in her sweater in an attempt to ward off the persistent chill in the air. Perhaps she ought to make the first move. It must be a lonely existence, living all on your own in your mother's house after she had passed away.

Yes, that was exactly what she should do: go over there and introduce herself. In time. Perhaps in the morning.

———— ◆ ————

The first night in her new home was oddly surreal.

After unpacking only the bare essentials, Leah had ordered a pizza and soon after crept into bed. She'd been tired, exhausted actually, but sleep still didn't find her.

Leah lay awake, staring at the ceiling for hours when a faraway noise had attracted her attention. Her flat in the city was right next to a railway line on one side and a busy road on the other, so silence was a luxury she had not been able to afford before.

This new place was exactly the opposite. The silence was deafening, making Leah take notice of every little creak and rustle that did manage to infiltrate her bedroom.

In the end, it was a click and squeak that roused her. The sound hadn't come from inside the house, but it was still too close to ignore. Leah grabbed a throw from the foot end of the bed and wrapped around herself and crept up to the window to see what was going on.

Next door, the light in the back yard was on, and she

could make out a shadowy movement through the gaps in the wooden fence separating her garden from Matthew Argyle's. As night had set in, it had apparently brought a mild fog with it, giving the entire scene a mysterious glow.

Why the hell would anyone be out in their garden at crazy o'clock at night? And in the freezing cold too!

Leah held her breath as she opened the window as quietly as she possibly could. The previously muffled sounds became clearer, and she could hear not just his footsteps, but also the occasional thump of heavy objects being set down on the soil, as well as metallic scratches. *Is he digging a hole?*

She remembered her earlier suspicions about the man, and simply couldn't stand not knowing what he was up to, barely ten feet away from her on the other side of that fence.

I can't sleep anyway; perhaps the fresh air will do me good...

Leah slipped on a pair of sneakers and exited through the back door. She again tried her best to be stealthy, walking on the grass instead of the pathway to dampen her steps. Within moments, she reached the same bit of fence visible from her bedroom window.

The activity on the other side had moved further away, but she could still hear Matthew pacing about.

Just a little peek...

Leah stepped up to the fence, her shoes sinking into the soft soil of the flower bed and looked through one of the many gaps between the wooden slats.

Although he had his back towards her, Leah felt validated in her nosiness already. As soon as she'd found out about her reclusive neighbor, a mental image had started to form. Her assumptions couldn't have been more wrong.

His broad shoulders, as well as deliberate movements with which he lifted one of the heavy paving slabs and carried it across his lawn didn't fit her expectations at all. He was strong to the extent that he made the hard labor look effortless.

In the dim light, as well as disguised by fog, Leah couldn't properly judge his wardrobe, but at least she could tell he wasn't wearing rags. His hair was closely cropped and thus looked neat enough. So he wasn't the unkempt spend-the-day-in-a-bathrobe type recluse at least.

And then he turned around.

Leah forgot to breathe and stumbled backward onto the lawn.

His strong jaw matched the rest of his physique. *Handsome* didn't quite describe him. And those eyes... A warm almost fiery amber, kind and yet infinitely sad.

That was the reason she'd stumbled in the first place. He seemed to be able to peek right into her soul, even though there was no reasonable way for him to even see her behind the fence. *Was there?*

As soon as she'd regained her composure, a confusing few seconds later, she was back at the fence, but her new neighbor was nowhere to be seen anymore.

Shame... Leah would have loved to catch another glimpse of him before heading back inside.

Despite everything, especially the mystery of why Matthew Argyle thought it appropriate to do a bit of landscaping in the middle of the night, her decision was final now. She was definitely going to make the first move and introduce herself the first chance she got.

CHAPTER THREE

The next day, Matt's doorbell rang, but he ignored it, instead keeping his head down and eyes locked onto the laptop screen. He never bothered with callers, unless he was expecting a delivery, so this wasn't unusual.

What was unusual was that for a change he knew exactly who stood there at the other side of his front door. It was the woman. He could feel her presence, just like last night. And that simple fact still didn't make any sense to him.

But then again, a lot of things in Matt's world didn't make sense. Like why the majority of the people on the discussion forum he'd posted on at night thought he should just be honest with her. What did they know?

He rubbed his eyes, but the alphabets on his screen continued to dance around in front of him. There was no way he could concentrate.

"I'm sorry to disturb. I'm new in the neighborhood and just wanted to say hello," she said. He could just about hear her muffled voice even though he was as far back inside the house as he possibly could be.

That was nice of her, but he couldn't risk it. Just the sound of her was putting him on edge. The hairs on his arms and legs were already standing up straight, readying themselves to grow.

"Anyway, perhaps you're busy, so I'm just going to leave this here," she continued.

Wait, leave what where? He got up and walked out of his office heading towards the entrance hall, then stopped in his tracks. What was he doing? If he got any closer, she'd see him and know he was avoiding her!

He waited, holding his breath until finally he heard footsteps move away from the door and down the steps of his porch. Another five minutes later, he finally dared to open the curtain of the porch window just enough to see outside. There was a basket on his foot mat. Of course, he couldn't tell what was inside from here.

It was still light out, and he had no way of knowing whether he was being watched, so he closed the curtain again and turned around to get back to work. But knowing that there was something out there, something *she* was trying to give him... He had to know what it was.

Barely an hour later, he'd again tried and failed to finish the article he'd begun writing that morning. Instead, he'd been reading and re-reading the reactions to his post on the discussion forum.

'If she's worthy, she'll accept you.' *Rubbish.*

'Wouldn't it be worse to always wonder *what if?'* *Ugh!*

The worst part was they were probably right in their own way. And he couldn't ignore that basket any longer without losing his mind completely, so he gave in to temptation. He returned to the front door, making sure through the curtain that nobody was around, and retrieved it.

A sweet sort of scent hung about it, and it wasn't just from the food he knew to be inside. Inside, he found a piece of heavy paper the size of a business card, a bar of soap that smelled of Christmas and a stack of carefully wrapped butter shortbread with a red ribbon tied around it.

Hello.

Matt turned the card over in his hand, hoping for something more, but that's all it said. Weird.

Seriously? You're the one who didn't even open the door for her, and you think this *is weird?*

It was still nice of her, though. Matt untied the ribbon

holding the shortbread together and took a bite. *Amazing.*

Only then did he take a closer look at the rustically shaped soap. It didn't seem shop bought and along with the cinnamon and hints of orange peel, there was a strong scent of something else in there as well. *Her. No, it can't be, can it?*

The material of the label was identical to the very concise card, which should have been the first thing for him to notice if he hadn't been so distracted.

On the sticker on the back, there was a website and a phone number.

When he pulled up the website on his laptop, he had to smile. This was actually quite clever. On the face of it, she'd just packed together a couple of things, little gifts. But between the lines, there was so much to learn. He couldn't help but assume that she'd done it this way deliberately.

As the site loaded, her picture greeted him from the right-hand column. She looked even more beautiful in it than he could have guessed from the short glimpse he'd caught of her yesterday. So she made soaps. That explained a lot.

He'd always had a keen sense of smell, as well as a whole other host of instincts that often overwhelmed. One of them was a tendency to see mysteries and secrets everywhere. Why had she even tried to make contact? Why give him anything in the first place?

Last night had been fairly easy to explain away: he was out making noise in the middle of the night, and she came to the fence to investigate. Simple. But this was something entirely different. Perhaps his strange night time activities had made her curious to find out more. She must be wondering what sort of a person she's ended up living next to; that was only natural.

Still...

Matt's brain wouldn't stop speculating.

He pushed the basket and its contents to the side and

focused on his laptop once more. What if these people were right? Maybe he should just get over himself already.

Her website was still open in the background. Her smile was radiant and inviting. He hovered over the speech bubble labeled 'get in touch' underneath her picture for a moment and found that he'd clicked it without consciously deciding so.

What to write? Seeing as she'd kept things very simple, he ought to do the same.

Hello & Thanks.

A rush of excitement passed through him as he hit 'send.' What if she doesn't realize who it was from? Again, a stupid thought... If it reached her, she would know.

That last thought was what allowed him to go back to his original plan for the day: the articles he was supposed to submit the next day. It was just as well that a reply wasn't forthcoming.

———— ♦ ————

Ever since Leah saw the short message in her inbox from a certain "M. A.", she couldn't help feeling some sense of accomplishment. She didn't know the man, obviously, but somehow she could tell that simply sending her a 'hello' back was a big step. She wasn't even sure why she cared, considering she had moved there in search for a simpler life, not a more complicated one.

Trying to strike up a conversation with a reclusive, yet rather attractive neighbor definitely counted as complicated.

Still, she couldn't help feeling pleased. He had responded, so the lines were now open, sort of. Unless he was just trying to be polite...

Despite thinking about what to do or say next for most of the day, there was plenty of work to be getting on with.

An engineer turned up to connect her TV, phone and broadband which took up the better part of the morning.

She was glad to no longer to have to rely on the rather patchy mobile signal. There was no network in her bedroom, bathroom, or most of the lounge; she'd learned that pretty quickly. Only along the front windows and in her kitchen did her mobile work properly.

Once the telecoms guy had gone, she had to start working through a couple of orders, necessitating a trip to the nearby post office. And then there were the boxes... the never-ending boxes that needed to be unpacked.

Only by the evening did she have the time as well as peace of mind to reply.

I'm Leah. Nice to "meet' you.

Send.

She was about to put her phone down on the coffee table and settle into the freshly fluffed up cushions on her couch to watch some TV when it dinged. That was fast! Almost as if he'd been waiting...

Matt, likewise. I saw you move in.

It wasn't much as a response, but it was something. Had he been watching her? Oh crap, what if he asked about her peeping through the fence at night? That would be so awkward! Perhaps it would be best to face that particular topic head-on...

Leah typed out her next response with trembling fingers. *Fingers crossed he won't take offense!*

So I guess you like gardening? I'm more indoorsy, a city girl.

Did that sound stupid? Too late now... Leah sent the email and waited, holding her breath.

You seemed pretty **outdoorsy last night...**

They say it's hard to catch the intent behind written words, but Leah was sure she could sense the dry humor in his observation. *Oh hell, if you want to play it like that!*

It was short-lived. I changed my mind once my toes started to turn blue.

Although she thought herself quite witty upon sending the mail, she wasn't so sure when nothing happened for a few minutes. Why wasn't he responding? She placed the phone next to her on the sofa and switched the TV on. Perhaps she'd missed the point of his message completely and turned him off.

While flipping through the channels, her phone finally lit up again with a notification. She bit her lip as she opened it.

Check the same spot.

What the hell? What was he talking about?

Leah crossed her lounge and headed straight to the bedroom window overlooking the place where she'd stumbled at night. Sure enough... the same basket she'd left on his doorstep was waiting there, a string attached to its handle.

She put on a coat - dusk was setting, and she'd only been half joking about the blue toes - and went out. Inside the basket was a stem of fragrant flowers; they looked somewhat like the orchids you can buy at the supermarket, but somehow more elegant. Underneath it awaited a bottle of red wine.

Leah stepped up closer to the boundary and looked through the gaps in the wood like she'd done the previous night, but there was no sign of movement on the other side. He must not be looking for an in-person chat.

Okay then... Clutching her prize in one hand, she also retreated and upon returning inside she picked up her phone again.

Cheers :)

She was about to send just that, then changed her mind.

... Do you have Whatsapp? It seems odd chatting via email.

Now she sent it. Again it took a little while for a response to arrive, giving Leah the chance to open one of the boxes waiting in the kitchen and take out a wine glass. This time, she wasn't worried anymore. Her new neighbor had turned out a lot more agreeable than she'd expected.

Sure enough, the next message was a positive one:

Now I do :)

Leah wasn't sure whether it was the wine or just the thrill of having broken the ice, but from then on conversation flowed a lot more freely. She learned that Matt was a freelance writer, which enabled him to work exclusively from home. In turn, she shared some of her work history, how she'd slogged through years at a call center in the city while dreaming of becoming her own boss.

It was nice to talk to someone in a similar position; after all, freelancing wasn't all that different from selling stuff online, not if you looked at the basics. You might set your own hours, but you're still dependent on clients ordering stuff, no matter if it's an article or a scented candle. And in both lines of work, word of mouth was everything.

Time flew as they continued to talk. Before she knew it,

the gifted bottle was mostly empty, and the clock showed 3 am. She hadn't even realized that the muted TV in front of her had been showing infomercials, probably for hours.

By the time they said good night, the former stranger next door had started to feel a lot like a friend.

CHAPTER FOUR

When Matt awoke, a little later than normal, it was with a smile on his face. He'd taken a chance, responded to Leah's little gift package, and as a result, spent the better part of the night talking to a real actual human being. Sure, it had been via email and chat, but this wasn't some anonymous person on a forum, but someone who was right there across the fence in the house next door.

And yeah, if he was being totally honest with himself, he could have talked to real people otherwise also. There were the neighbors he'd grown up with, who probably would be happy to have a chat with him, but this was different. They knew the old him. They had expectations he wasn't able to live up to anymore.

Leah hadn't known him before. She only knew what he'd told her. And for some reason he couldn't quite fathom, she hadn't told him to go away and leave her alone. She'd interacted with him like normal people did with each other. Except in writing.

He'd never had any use for chat apps, but installed one on his phone at her request, and he was glad to have done so. It was a lot easier to carry a phone around the house than his laptop.

Looking at it now, lying on the table beside his bed, he was tempted to pick it up and wish her good morning. Did people do that? Would that be weird?

He resisted for now, getting up and making himself a cup of coffee instead.

Outside, life was going on as normal. Kids were leaving their homes and grouping together in the street with their bicycles, ready to head to school. The garbage truck was making its usual round through the neighborhood.

And next door, a familiar silhouette was walking to her

car carrying half a dozen little parcels. Leah.

He leaned across the kitchen counter and lifted the curtain aside to get a better look. She must have gotten a few more orders overnight. Good. He hoped for her business to work out. She seemed like a smart, ambitious woman who deserved a break after years in a crappy job.

Funny. Only yesterday he dreaded seeing her around because it would just lead to him obsessing about her, but overnight she had become a welcome, even familiar sight. He couldn't look away if he wanted to.

The way the wind tussled her hair made him smile again. She tried her best to brush one particularly stubborn lock behind her ear using just her upper arm but was unsuccessful and dropped a couple of parcels in the process.

He should go out there and help her out.

Of course, he didn't, but he ought to. In his place, someone else came up to Leah and picked up the fallen packets. Permed blond hair and tightly fitted velvet tracksuit: Carrie, who had lived two doors down from Matt pretty much forever.

If only he could overhear the conversation taking place outside.

It wasn't that he disliked Carrie; it was just that the woman she had grown into was nothing like the little girl he'd played tag with in the past. She'd followed in her mother's footsteps and had become the main source of gossip in the neighborhood.

Matt didn't appreciate gossip, especially since he expected to be the topic of it more often than not. Nothing ever happened in Gartcosh that was worth talking about, so why not discuss the crazy guy who never left home?

The two women glanced over in Matt's direction, Leah with what looked like the subtlest of smiles on her face while Carrie's expression was hard with suspicion. Were they talking about him?

Leah finished loading her things into the backseat of her little car, while Carrie kept loitering around. Matt breathed a sigh of relief when Leah finally sat in the driver's seat and left.

He should remember to tell her to be cautious around Carrie. Whatever she told her would be shared with the whole village soon after. That woman had no sense of boundaries.

Carrie glanced over at him one last time then turned around to head back home. Matt also let go of the curtain and prepared himself for a productive day ahead. Hopefully, come nightfall, there'd be more conversation to look forward to. He'd be ready just in case.

———•———

It had only been a couple of days since the move, but Leah was starting to feel at home already. The place was perfect, just big enough to be able to house all her supplies as well as stock, yet small enough to be cozy for just one person.

Leah turned the key with a smile on her face and admired her new living room. Everything was set up just how she wanted it. All the boxes were unpacked, all the paintings hung and framed pictures lined up on the mantle. If her dad could see the place right now, he'd be proud.

She glanced down at the phone in her hand. She'd been carrying the thing around all day obsessively, hoping for a message from Matt. A bit needy perhaps?

Still, she hadn't imagined the two nights in a row that they'd spent exchanging stories and random thoughts. It was nothing like her previous relationship, which had been with a man who had the emotional maturity of a clam. Matt was different.

Perhaps it was that they were communicating in writing, which made the two of them open up so much more than they might have in person. They'd shared stories of past loves and other things she'd never told anyone she'd only just met, especially not a guy. Perhaps they'd found it easy to connect because they'd both grown up in a single-parent household?

Body language was a wonderful, yet often distracting thing. It was interesting to do without it for a while. In the case of a guy like Matt, who was unnervingly handsome in person, it was probably a good thing she couldn't see him while "talking" to him.

Ever since Leah had started her online business, the ding of her phone would get her just a little bit excited. It could be a customer enquiry, or better yet, a new order. But none of that could compare to the thrill she felt when she saw a new message from Matt. He definitely had made an impact, though she couldn't be sure that feeling was mutual.

In fact, there came another message, the first one of the day: "Had a good day?"

Leah smiled as she typed out her response. "Yes indeed. Getting the hang of the local geography. Did you know there's a charming little antique shop right there by the village green? It's so cute I nearly died."

Leah carried her purchases, mostly groceries, into the kitchen and waited.

"No kidding? Isn't that where the post office used to be?" Matt replied.

She shook her head and let out a chuckle.

"You need to get out more. It's next door to the post office." As soon as she'd sent her response, Leah's heart sank. Did she honestly just write that to him? Oh, crap.

"You're funny. Maybe next time. ;-)" Thank God, he hadn't taken offense. Leah breathed a sigh of relief. Perhaps body language wasn't so overrated after all.

"It's a date," Leah replied, her heart fluttering just a little bit. She wasn't quite sure why, but for some reason, she had this irresistible urge to get flirty with him. This was the most overt attempt so far, though. How would he respond?

"In that case: flowers or chocolate?"

Leah bit her lip. He has taken the bait.

"Do I have to pick just one?" she asked in response.

"Right you are. You don't. A girl like you deserves both."

She was speechless for a moment. She'd started it, but now they'd both crossed that invisible line in the sand. They were no longer just neighbors being friendly. There was something else going on here, and it felt good.

"You know where I live :-)" Leah couldn't stop smiling. This new life of hers was shaping up to be quite exciting indeed.

"Flowers and chocolates for the lady. That can certainly be arranged."

"And don't think you can get away with just smooth talking me. I'll be heartbroken if you don't follow through. :-)"

"No worries. I'm a man of my word."

Leah felt like hugging her phone but resisted at the last moment. She wasn't a teenager anymore after all.

Was he as excited as she was right now? Maybe. Hopefully. Perhaps she should ask him. No, that would be a dumb attempt to look behind the curtain and ruin the magic.

Still, though, this thing with Matt made her feel good about herself. Ever since planning to set out on her own, she hadn't given herself permission to date. The baggage left over from the last man in her life had also played a part. Perhaps this thing, this weird long-distance type deal with the man next door was exactly what she needed.

It's easy to convince yourself you don't need anyone when everyone tells you you're crazy to leave your job. But Matt had been supportive, something Leah hadn't realized she'd wanted, and yet he wasn't about to take over her whole life to the extent that she would no longer be able to achieve her business goals. He might not be Mr. Perfect, but whatever was developing here sure seemed to fit perfectly into Leah's life.

She plopped down on the sofa and started typing again. Now that this initial hurdle had been crossed, there was a whole lot more for the both of them to talk about. The night was still young, and she didn't want to miss a moment of it.

CHAPTER FIVE

Leah had come home late. The custom order that had come in earlier in the day for two hundred spring themed wedding favor bags meant a trip into the city for supplies was in order.

She didn't mind the drive so much, nor the traffic, because she knew that at the end of the day she had a quiet home to retreat to. Hers wasn't a city life anymore.

So when she unlocked the door and stepped inside, she could breathe a sigh of relief. Here she was, away from the noise and confusion. Here she could relax.

Leah started to unpack her shopping. The much needed supplies were put away for later in favor of the groceries she needed right this moment. She popped a ready meal into the microwave and poured herself a glass of wine while waiting.

One of these days, she'd decide to learn how to cook from scratch as well, but not today. Leah had more pressing things to occupy herself with, such as messaging Matt, which had become a welcome ending to every day since they started talking shortly after she'd moved into the place.

"What a day," Leah started the conversation

"Oh yeah?" Matt responded instantly, as usual.

"I'd almost forgotten how busy the city can be."

"I wouldn't know. Cities aren't my thing."

"Anyway, glad to be back home. I'm enjoying a ready made lasagna."

"Say what? Sawdust with cheese on top?"

"We can't all be awesome cooks like you."

"Can't or won't?"

Typical. Won't leave the house but has opinions about everything. Leah let out a chuckle, then opened the camera app and took a close-up of her plate.

"If you serve it up nicely before eating, you can't tell the difference," she wrote as a caption to the picture.

"Wanna bet?" Matt wrote, along with a photograph of a very inviting looking steak covered in creamy peppercorn sauce. Damn. He was right, of course.

"Trying to make me jealous? Watch it, or I'm coming over there demanding a share," Leah responded, only half joking. Their daily exchanges had progressed from innocent small talk to merciless teasing and flirtations. What would happen if he allowed things to progress to the logical next step?

Would she be as comfortable with him in person? Perhaps... Or perhaps the chemistry they felt was limited only to characters on a screen.

"What makes you think there'd be any left?" Matt responded. Something told her that the day he let his guard down and allowed her in closer, there would be. But he wasn't ready yet, and she wasn't about to force things.

"Anyway, I stopped by this new micro-brewery on the way home. If you're nice, I might leave you a bottle," Leah wrote.

"I'm always nice."

Ha!

"Give me a moment while I sort out the kitchen. BRB." Leah put the phone down and got to work. The advantage of not actually cooking was that there wasn't much to tidy away afterward either. Soon she was done and keen to properly relax with a second glass of Merlot.

Leah retrieved the phone, switched off the living room lights and retreated to her bedroom. As comfortable as the living area was, her bedroom was her safe haven. It helped that it was also the part of the house closest to Matt.

"Okay, I'm back," Leah restarted the chat.

"You want to watch a movie together? Tune in to Channel 4."

Leah frowned; this was new, but why the hell not? She

didn't have a TV in the bedroom, but then again she didn't need one. The Internet had everything, even live TV.

"Dracula?" Leah asked.

"What's wrong with Dracula? This version is a classic."

"All right then, just checking." Leah settled into her pillows and wrapped a throw around her shoulders. The air in the bedroom was chillier than the living room, but soon that wouldn't matter anymore.

In between sips of wine, and the odd comment or remark, Leah soon became immersed in the movie. It had been ages since she'd seen it last. The first time around, she'd dismissed it as silly and a bit camp. This time, though, something spoke to her; she could feel the attraction. How tempting it might be to give in to the darkness, to get close to a man (or vampire) so dangerous.

It was because he'd suggested it, and they were watching together, even though they were apart probably. That was what made her enjoy the film. Maybe one day they'd be in the same room, the same bed even? Leah could only hope so.

As the movie came to a climax, something sent a chill down Leah's spine. A noise. A clicking sound had disturbed her that hadn't come from the speakers on her tablet. She muted it and listened out for more.

"Hey, I just heard something," Leah typed.

"What?"

"A noise-" Leah barely managed to write that much when another, louder sound cut through the silence. Shit. This was definitely close, maybe even inside the house.

She wrapped the throw tighter around herself and got up to investigate. Years living on her own in the city had made her cautious, but she wasn't a wimp. Like that one time someone burgled the flat next to hers while her neighbor was out. She'd heard the whole thing and called the police just in time.

Damn. Footsteps. She didn't even have anything to defend herself with! Hiding was the only remaining option.

Leah snatched the phone from the mattress and got underneath the bed. Zero bars, all she had was the Wifi. So much for that plan. She opened Whatsapp again.

"There's someone in the house," she messaged. "I don't have a network. Call for help." Her bedroom door creaked open just after she managed to send the final message. She tightly pressed the phone against her chest and held her breath. Her heart was beating so hard it was all she could hear.

Maybe they won't find her. Maybe...

She let out a short shriek when a hand closed around her ankle and pulled her backward.

———◆———

Matt stared at his phone for a second. Call for help? Was this some kind of weird joke?

He didn't get much time to analyze the situation. A distant scream pierced through his entire being. It wasn't loud, and he doubted any other neighbor would have heard it. *Her voice. This was real. Shit.*

His body sprang into action before his mind did, and the transformation was over within a fraction of a second, leaving his clothes on the floor in tatters. It didn't matter what shape he was supposedly in; he knew he had to step up. There was no way he'd let her down.

Although he'd never been in any sort of scenario like this, instinct kicked in. If he charged in there without a strategy, this whole thing could end badly for the both of them. Instead, he opted for stealth.

He checked through the kitchen window, looking for any sign of activity. All seemed quiet now, except for a shadowy figure, loitering around Leah's front steps. There was no way he could get in without tipping this person off.

Matt headed for the backyard instead, opening his back door as quietly as he possibly could and listening for movement on the other side of the fence. Nothing. A quick check through the wooden slats suggested all was clear. This was to be his entry point.

With swift movements, he picked up his heavy wooden picnic table and placed it beside the boundary, before climbing on top and jumping over the top of the six-foot-tall fence, landing in the soft grass and crouching down immediately for cover.

There was no way anyone could have heard him unless they had the same super sensitive hearing he had. Looking down, the sight of massive furry paws where his hands should have been was distracting, but not enough to throw him off track. It's just a trick of the mind.

Some light filtered through the gap in the curtains, revealing two silhouettes standing across from one another. They seemed to be arguing, but he couldn't make out the words, so he crawled ahead and crouched underneath the window.

"She's just a human. We can't do this!" a younger sounding male voice whispered.

"She said this was the place. You've got to learn to follow orders, soldier!" this voice sounded older, more authoritative.

"But..."

"Decide quickly where your loyalties lie. With the Sons or the scum we're hunting. Because if you're not with me now, I'm going to take it very personally."

"Fine. Let's do this."

Shit, what exactly is it they're planning on doing with Leah? This didn't seem to be a regular break-in. For whatever reason, these people targeted Leah's house on purpose. But why?

"All right missy, you're coming with us," the younger guy barked.

Leah let out a muffled squeal.

"If you behave, we can take the gag off. Understand?"

She didn't react, or at least, she wasn't vocal about it. There was a pause.

"What do you want from me?" Leah whispered at last.

"Don't play dumb. You must have known this could happen - that we could turn up."

"I don't know what you're talking about!" Leah argued.

"Stop it, or I'll gag you again."

What the hell was all this about? Had Leah been hiding something? Perhaps there was a reason she'd abruptly moved out of the city and into this house. Not that it mattered, of course, Matt owed it to her, as well as himself to do something about this.

He got up just far enough to be able to see inside. Luckily, the darkness gave him a good amount of cover so the intruders inside wouldn't be able to spot him.

The two men stood off to one side, again discussing something or other, then the older one headed out the bedroom door, leaving behind his uncertain companion, and Leah, of course.

This was Matt's chance.

He got up and checked the window. He could just about get one of his claws underneath the bottom edge. It would give; he was sure of it.

Given the element of surprise was on his side, he could make it. He had to make it.

Matt gave it his all, pulling at the window, which opened up even more easily than he'd foreseen and jumped into Leah's bedroom in one swift move. The man swung around; his face turning white as a sheet when he saw Matt.

"Fu-" he exclaimed, but Matt didn't give him the chance to finish, instead disabling him with a strong blow to the chest.

Then he turned to check on Leah, who looked equally shocked. She was even more beautiful close up than he had dared to imagine. If only the circumstances of their first proper meeting had been better.

"Please..." she whispered, her voice completely choked with fear. "Shit."

"Don't worry. I'll keep you safe," Matt said, but it was no use. He could tell from Leah's expression that his words weren't getting through to her at all. In fact, she'd started trembling all over. Seeing her this way cut right into his core.

He wanted to console her, to convince her that everything would be fine now. But there was no time to worry about that, because the door swung open, revealing the guy who'd seemed to be in charge of the strange operation.

"I knew it! This is the right house," he said only partly triumphantly, while holding up both his hands as if surrendering and backing out of the doorway into the hallway. His right hand twitched subtly before reaching for something. Matt didn't want to find out what, instead charging for the guy and pinning him down onto the ground.

The second kidnapper hit the floor so fast it knocked him out instantly.

Two down, one to go.

But Matt never got the chance to take care of the third guy. Instead, he was faced with the last thing he ever expected to see: Another great big brown bear, flanked by a smaller, blackish one. What the hell?

"Matthew Argyle, I presume?" the first bear seemed to say. How ludicrous. Bears can't talk. And how would he know his name anyway? This wasn't even Matt's house.

"Uhh..." That was all Matt could utter. What in the world was going on? Had he finally lost his mind completely?

"Looks like we got here just in time," the smaller one, a female, remarked. Her snippy tone rubbed Matt the wrong way, no matter how bizarre the situation was.

"I had it under control," Matt stammered.

"I can see that," the female responded.

"Please come with us," the bigger male said. He had an inherent authority hanging around him, but Matt wasn't so easily deterred.

"I've got to check on Leah," Matt explained as if that would make these two figments of his imagination vanish into thin air, allowing him to focus once more on the task at hand.

But they didn't vanish. Instead, they exchanged a look and almost instantly morphed into humans. Very naked humans.

The man snipped his fingers, and, from the other end of the hallway, someone flung a couple of bundles of clothes at them, which they swiftly put on.

Jeez, how many of them were there?

"You're just going to stay like this, are you?" the woman, who looked a lot less distracting now that she was wearing a pair of cargo pants and a black pullover, asked.

"Who are you people exactly? And why are you here?" Matt responded, ignoring her odd question.

"I guess a thank you was too much to ask. Be glad we came when we did, or these clowns-" The woman nodded at the kidnapper who was still lying at Matt's paws. "Would have taken you and the human woman as soon as their backup arrived."

Backup? What the hell was she talking about?

"Oh, you didn't think it was just the two of them and another standing guard, did you?" she asked.

"That's enough. Matthew. You'll have questions. We'll answer them to the best of our knowledge, but only once we get back to base. Margaret here will ensure your lady friend is all taken care of. All right?" the man took over.

"Okay..." Matt frowned. Margaret, eh? That name really didn't suit her; it seemed too old fashioned.

"I'm Henry, by the way. Let's go then."

The black-haired woman, Margaret, resolutely marched off into Leah's bedroom, and soon the two of them could be heard talking. Perhaps these guys were real then, not imagined.

Matt finally gave in and allowed himself to be escorted

through the hallway and lounge and out of the house, where a bunch of dejected looking skinheads stood around with their wrists tied together, surrounded by even more big men and a couple of women wearing black commando gear.

Every single head turned in Matt's direction when he stepped out into the street. It was nightmarish, and hair- no, fur-raising.

"That's really him, isn't it?" someone whispered behind Matt.

"Yeah. He's been missing for so long everyone thought he was dead."

Were they talking about him? How did these people even know anything about him? He needed to find out exactly the how and whys of today's events; that was the only reason he was going along with these people. And Leah... he couldn't wait to come back and talk to her. In person.

CHAPTER SIX

It had to have been a dream. A crazy, surreal, impossible dream.

Leah kept watching the woman- she'd introduced herself as Margaret - as she spoke, but her words weren't getting through to her at all.

One moment, Leah had been remotely watching a movie with Matt, the next all hell had broken loose. Who the hell were the two men who had come into her house and tried to take her? What possible reason could they have had? They seemed to know something she didn't.

And who were the people who intervened, including this Margaret woman who had stayed back to talk to her? She'd introduced herself as being from some kind of covert police task force, but Leah found that hard to believe.

"It's strange, how our mind tries to trick us, isn't it?" Margaret asked.

"What? Oh, yeah, very strange," Leah mumbled, averting her gaze from Margaret's prying eyes.

Margaret continued to speak, and Leah made sure to nod and voice her agreement in all the right places. She was being handled, just like her supervisor in her old job used to do when she wanted Leah to take on more work for the same pay. Much like her supervisor, Leah could tell Margaret wasn't used to having someone disagree with her either, so it would be easier - and quicker - to just agree to anything she said while letting her own thoughts run rampant inside her head.

If the entire home invasion part of tonight wasn't bad enough, Leah couldn't get one particular image out of her head. The bear.

She'd been terrified when the bear came in - after all,

who wouldn't be - but there was also something strangely familiar about it. She could swear there was something familiar in its eyes, something that had had a calming effect on her...But how could that be? She'd never seen a bear before, well, not outside of a zoo anyway, so how could she possibly have recognized it?

And then, if that wasn't weird enough, the bear hadn't attacked her. Instead, it had gone straight for the intruders in her house. As though it was trying to protect her. That wasn't possible either, though, was it?

After what felt like hours of nodding her head like a bobblehead to all sorts of explanations of stress induced hallucinations, Margaret finally left Leah to be alone with her thoughts.

Still shaky with the after-effects of her insane ordeal, Leah headed straight for the kitchen to make herself a cup of tea. No, better yet, something a bit stronger. The morning was early enough that it still counted as night, or at least, that's what she told herself. Propriety be damned; she needed a drink.

As she poured herself a stiff one - Scotch that had been in her possession for much too long, she realized there was something else she needed as much, if not more. Her phone.

Matt would have seen the commotion outside her home and be desperate for some kind of update. Leah knew she would be if she were in his place.

Drink in hand, Leah rushed back into her bedroom. Where was the damn thing? Under the bed! That's where she had it last. She got down on all fours and found it soon after. No unread messages. Nothing.

What the hell? The last thing she sent to him was a call for help. Wasn't he, at least, a little concerned?

Sure, their relationship - if you could call it that - wasn't exactly traditional, but she'd felt that he cared about her at least a little. Had she been kidding herself?

Had it all been in her head? The little flirtations, the

bond she'd felt toward him?

Then again, he wasn't anything like her previous lovers. He wasn't really normal, strictly speaking. Could she expect him to react like a normal guy would to an extraordinary situation like this? Perhaps not.

Leah took a deep breath, and a generous sip of the burning amber liquid she'd absentmindedly poured into a mug rather than a glass and decided to be the bigger person. She'd send him a message then.

I guess you're wondering what went on here tonight, eh?

Send.

Leah stared down at her phone for much too long, but nothing happened. There was no response, no matter how long she tried to hypnotize it.

Goddamnit. She had moved to this place in search for a simpler life. Two weeks in, she'd been the victim of a home invasion, come face-to-face with a life-sized bear inside her own home, undergone a weird brain-washing exercise courtesy of Margaret, who mysteriously showed up just around the same time as the bear.

And, to top it off, she'd developed a one-sided crush on someone she can't have. She had completely misread that situation. Bloody brilliant.

She threw the phone down onto the sofa in disgust and headed back into the kitchen. Through the windows, she could see that even the last one of the blacked out vans that had not too long ago been parked up outside her house had left, presumably taking Margaret with it. Good riddance.

As Leah poured herself another double, she wasn't shaken anymore; she was furious.

———— ♦ ————

An insomniac at the best of times, Leah hadn't even tried to go to bed that night, so come 8 o'clock, she was still up.

The buzz from the two shots of Scotch had worn off for the most part, and last night's events seemed very long ago.

She began doing the one thing that usually seemed to help when she had some issues to work through in her head: cook up a new batch of product. Funny, how she hadn't attempted to cook a meal for herself from scratch, but thought nothing of combining all these strange ingredients to produce soap.

She'd been telling herself for a while now that a new scent was required but just hadn't found the right combination of fragrances yet. Perhaps today was the day she'd figure it out.

Leah laid out all her essential oils, pairing them up in groupings she hadn't yet tried together, and put on a pair of gloves.

Although December had just begun, she didn't want to do anything Christmassy, so she quickly pushed aside the spicier scents.

Something fresh, new. That's what she was after. Like newly cut grass or the first flowers of spring. Daffodils? Why not...

She was just getting into the spirit of things when the doorbell rang and dragged her back into the real world. God. Hopefully, it wasn't that Margaret woman again.

Leah took a deep breath and rushed out to open the door only to find her other neighbor, Carrie, waiting outside. Just great. She'd probably seen the activity outside her door at night as well.

Matt had said she was a gossip - though, screw whatever Matt had told her.

"Hi!" Leah greeted Carrie with an attempt at a wide smile.

"Hey, Leah, how's it going?" Carrie couldn't quite disguise her curiosity. Her eyes clearly darted back and forth between Leah and the hallway behind her, as though she was looking for something or someone.

"Yeah, not too bad, considering. I suppose you must have seen a bit of what went on here at night?" Leah said, hoping to speed things up by steering the conversation in the direction she expected Carrie wanted to head in anyway.

"I did wake up to an awful ruckus outside. Cars pulling in, people running back and forth. I hope everything is okay?"

"Someone broke in; can you believe it?"

"No way! In this neighborhood?"

"That's what I thought. I still don't know what they were after. It was lucky the police showed up when they did, or I don't know what might have happened," Leah said.

Carrie's eyes widened at her mention of the police.

"So it was the police outside? I didn't hear sirens or anything."

"Standard procedure apparently, when the intruders are still in the house," Leah explained. "I was hiding under the bed when they came in." There was no way she was going to tell Carrie the truth, but she felt she had to give her something in order to get rid of her.

"Oh, my word! You must have been terrified!"

"Yeah, it was quite something. Say, you haven't had issues like this before, have you?"

"No, nothing like that. This has always been a very safe area," Carrie mumbled, obviously impressed by Leah's version of events. "Well, do let me know if you need anything. I'd better be off making sure the kids are dressed for school..."

Good. Leah smiled and nodded at Carrie as she said her goodbyes. Hopefully, that would be the first and last time she had to tell that particular story to anyone.

Leah wrapped her arms around herself against the chill still coming through her open front door. She'd changed things a bit, but her new version of events was so much more plausible than what had actually gone down, it actually felt a bit real.

She glanced over to the left, in the direction of Matt's place. Unbelievable that he still hasn't made contact. After everything that had happened.

Leah took a couple of steps outside and peeped across the low hedge separating their houses. His place looked dark - not that that was unusual - but just a bit darker than normal. As though he wasn't even home. But how could that be, when he himself had admitted to her that he never left his house?

Well anyway, if he wanted to hide himself away from her also, that was his problem, not hers. Leah took a deep breath, suppressing the sting in her chest that had first developed hours before when she'd messaged him and not had a response.

She shook her head and walked back inside, returning to the neatly lined up bottles of essential oils she'd left in her otherwise pristine kitchen. Sniffing the various combinations one by one, none of them seemed quite right.

No matter how hard she tried to concentrate, it was no use, though. Angry or hurt, she couldn't stop herself from feeling something. Something that affected her ability to work.

Alone. Yes, that was it. Out here in this new place that had turned out to be not as safe as she'd hoped; she suddenly felt very alone.

CHAPTER SEVEN

After a short drive in the back of a windowless van, Matt reached the supposed base; an old warehouse that looked somewhat like an impromptu command center from any generic espionage movie. Were these guys for real?

There was a lot of activity. Blindfolded and handcuffed men were being led through the warehouse and locked away somewhere in another part of the building. At the same time, the entire team of people involved in the action - they identified themselves as "the Alliance" - deposited weapons, communication equipment, and other items on their respective desks.

Matt took a seat at an unoccupied table and just observed. It was like a strange dream, like he had found himself in the middle of a Hollywood movie, and he was the only one aware that none of this was in any way normal.

As Matt looked around, his brain tried to make sense of it all. These people were like him. He'd seen it.

That meant that either all of them were as crazy as he was, or that his self-identified delusions were true. He'd convinced himself that the things he experienced were in his head for so long, it was near impossible to accept the opposite.

And what about Leah? She didn't know anything about this stuff, so she had to be even more confused than he was right now. To think he burst into her bedroom fully shifted... No wonder she'd been shocked. And he couldn't do a bloody thing about it!

"It's really you. I can't believe it," a voice spoke behind him.

Matt jumped up from his chair and turned to find a man with a vaguely familiar face stand before him. He reminded him of a very distant past. Could it be? He wanted to say something but couldn't find the right words.

"Matty! Shit, do you even remember me?" The man smiled, but his eyes didn't look happy.

"Jamie?" Matt asked after a few long seconds.

Relief washed over Jamie's face. "You do recognize me. I was worried. It's been such a long time, since..."

"What the hell is going on here?" Matt asked, but Jamie didn't get the chance to answer.

"Mr. Brown, is it? How wonderful to make your acquaintance." A slightly sinister looking middle-aged man wearing a suit reminiscent of 1920s gangster movies offered his hand to Matt. Where the hell had he come from? ? And how did he know his former name, a name he'd pretty much forgotten about himself?

"Blacke. Adrian Blacke."

"Uhh, my name's Matt Argyle, actually," Matt mumbled while exchanging a puzzled look with Jamie, who didn't seem too happy to see the strange man.

"It's so good to see a lost one of ours returned to his own people, don't you think, Abbott-" Why was he referring to Jamie by a different name as well? "Despite the trials of your difficult childhood, I trust you'll feel at home in no time at all." The man, Blacke, flashed a row of white, be-it crooked teeth.

"My childhood was fine," Matt remarked - his troubles didn't start until around his seventeenth birthday - but Blacke wasn't listening. Instead, he waved at Jamie, taking him aside and leaving Matt standing on his own just out of earshot.

Matt observed the conversation while instinctively reaching into his right pocket. Empty. Damn, he should ask Jamie about his phone.

As the chat in front of Matt went on, it became obvious that Jamie didn't like this Blacke character much at all, and Matt couldn't blame him. The man had a strange vibe around him which Matt didn't appreciate either.

It took a few more minutes for Jamie to return, sporting a tense expression on his face.

"Is everything okay?" Matt asked.

"Blacke wants you to stay here for a while until I can arrange something for you locally."

"Arrange what?"

"A place, whatever. I told him you could just come back to Edinburgh with me, but-"

"Why do I need a new place? And what were those skinheads trying to do exactly?"

Jamie scrutinized him for a moment. "You mean, you want to go back? To the house they held you prisoner in?"

"What are you talking about? I wasn't held prisoner anywhere!" Matt felt himself getting riled up, causing his skin to tingle again, ready for another transformation.

"But they took you, from the beach, when we were kids," Jamie argued.

"That may be so, but Molly raised me as her own. I was never locked up or anything." Deep breaths. Calm down. Don't tear this new change of clothes as well.

"Then why didn't you try to escape, to come back to us?" Jamie asked.

"Dude, I was eight. After Mom and Dad died-"

"What do you mean Mom and Dad died?! They're not dead!"

Matt was shocked into silence for a moment. "That was a lie... Of course. A lie to get me to go along with them willingly." He sighed, relieved to feel his muscles relax before the unthinkable would happen again. "Okay, I think we have a lot of catching up to do."

"Indeed," Jamie agreed.

They didn't get the chance for it just yet, because, at that moment, the large bear/human who had intervened at the house turned up. Henry.

"Matt." Henry offered his hand. "Good to see you in your usual form."

Matt accepted the man's handshake and nodded. It felt

good to be back to his normal self as well.

"I see your family reunion is well underway. I must say, when Jamie came to me with the information that you'd been located, I wasn't sure what to expect, but I never expected to capture so many of our enemies as well."

Enemies? Oh, he must be talking about the guys who had come to take Leah.

"Yeah, I'm not quite sure what went on there. I was hoping you guys had some insights to share."

"Perhaps we'll know more after our interrogations." Henry shrugged off Matt's question. *Just great.*

But, of course, that wasn't the only thing Matt was keen to learn about. As soon as Henry walked off again, he took the time to question Jamie about anything and everything that popped into his head.

That was how he found out that he was indeed a bear. A werebear - as was almost everyone in the Alliance, except for the odd werewolf here and there who had joined the fight. He learned about who the Alliance really was, that Jamie was in charge of a group of them in Edinburgh, and about their shared enemy, the Sons of Domnall. Slowly but surely the new information allowed Matt to piece together what must have happened to him when he was just a kid.

The one thing he couldn't figure out was how Leah had gotten involved in this mess. Nothing in her reaction to his shifted self suggested she knew anything about what was going on. Even the main intruder's reaction to seeing Matt's bear form suggested it was him they were after, not her, which made very little sense. If it was the Sons of Domnall who had arranged for Matt's abduction as a child, then why did they break into the wrong house?

"It goes without saying that it's best not to repeat any of this to anyone. I mean anyone human," Jamie said after answering Matt's last question.

"Why?"

"It's one of our most important rules. If the human

world came to know about us, well... you can imagine what would happen. That's why we don't even tell our own children until they're old enough to understand."

Matt certainly could imagine people would be shocked; Leah certainly had been. Shit, surely he could be honest with *her*, couldn't he? Then again, if he had known about any of this, his adult life might have been very different. It was only because of all the secrecy surrounding their kind that he had assumed all of this was in his head and started to pull away from everyone around him.

Perhaps it would have been better to get everything out in the open. It might help someone in his position... Still, he wasn't sure he could trust Jamie with everything going on in his head. He was his brother, sure, but he didn't really know him anymore, did he?

"So what if one of us, a bear, for example, hypothetically, were to get involved with a regular human? Then what?"

Jamie gave him a suspicious look. "I see. The woman whose house you were in..."

"Theoretically," Matt emphasized.

"It wouldn't be wise for someone like us to get involved with one of them. It would be reckless and stupid."

Matt heard Jamie's words, but his tone didn't sound convinced. There was something his brother wasn't telling him.

"The only way to be with a human is to live like a human. To deny the bear inside you. Of course, it tends to want to claw its way to the surface in a lot of us, so I'm not sure that would really work."

"Uhuh."

Jamie looked around the room, and then leaned in closer to Matt.

"How serious is it?"

"As I said, I was just giving an example."

"Bullshit, I can see it in your eyes. I know-" Jamie

paused when one of the females on the team walked past. "I'm not supposed to tell you this, but to hell with it, you're my little brother, and nobody else can guide you right now... I get it. Really, I do."

Matt waited while Jamie took a deep breath and continued. "We're in the same boat, you and I. I too have developed feelings for a human woman. It happens. And it is unwise like I said. If Blacke found out..."

"Blacke, right." Matt scanned the room, looking for the man in the three-piece suit. "He wouldn't approve?"

"We'd be in a whole lot of trouble. The Alliance council is very strict when it comes to protecting our secrets and with it the safety of our people. They would stop at nothing..."

"Okay, so what do we do?"

"Nothing. Do what your gut tells you to do, but for fuck's sake, don't tell anyone anything about what you're up to. By now Margaret will have assessed the situation, and probably convinced your girlfriend that she's been seeing things, and none of it really happened. You'd better hope she agreed to that version of events."

Damn. Matt dreaded to think what would happen if she didn't.

"What did you do? You told your girl about who you really are?" Matt asked.

"It's a long story; she already knew. But Blacke must never find out."

"I understand." Clearly, there was a lot left to be said, but this wasn't the time or the place. First, Matt had to focus on getting out of here without setting off too many alarm bells. He had to get back to Leah at any cost.

Suddenly, in just one evening, his entire life had changed. He'd left his house for the first time in years, found out about his true nature, and come face-to-face with the woman he'd been obsessing about for weeks. Finally, there was a chance there, a hope. If only she could accept him.

"Matt. I know what you're thinking, but you're not ready," Jamie interrupted his thoughts.

"What?"

"You've first got to learn how to control this thing. They'll never let you out there if you randomly shift without intending to. It's too risky. You could expose all of us."

He didn't want to hear it, but Jamie was right. He had to sort himself out. He could only hope that by the end of it, Leah would still be there, waiting for him.

CHAPTER EIGHT

The room was cold, uninviting, which was exactly the point. Matt felt his skin tighten with every breath, and it was difficult, no, near impossible to stay in control.

But Jamie didn't let up. He kept goading him, kept attacking. It had started off as a simulated boxing match just like yesterday's training, but today Jamie had taken things just a little bit further.

"You've got to withstand the urge, little brother," he taunted him while stepping forward, trying to get a right hook in. He was wearing gloves, but Matt's instincts didn't know that.

Sure enough, as soon as the leather hit the side of his face, Matt's back started to sprout fur, and a growl escaped his lips.

"That's not holding back, in fact, that's pretty much the opposite," Jamie remarked.

Matt balled his fists, but the feeling didn't subside. How could anyone battle the red fog that tried its best to overwhelm him? It didn't make sense.

"Take a deep breath, focus on something that relaxes you," Jamie added.

Matt closed his eyes and inhaled sharply. The cold air stung against the inside of his nostrils, reminding him of just the place. Applecross Bay, where they used to come as kids. The air was fresh there too.

The sensation subsided, so he opened his eyes again, just in time to see Jamie's other gloved fist fly at his face. That did it. Matt's body twisted and morphed, and within a split second, he was no longer the half-naked man, shivering against the cold of his cell, but a magnificent beast, towering over Jamie's still human self.

"Enough!" Matt growled, his right paw raised in the air

as though he was about to strike.

Jamie lifted his gloves up in defeat. "Fine. How about we take a break, huh?"

Almost instantly, Matt's limbs and torso contracted again, and the fur made way for smooth skin once more.

"I gotta tell you, if you keep going through clothes like that, we're going to run out," Jamie remarked, nodding down at the pile of torn fabric on the floor.

Damn . Matt averted his gaze. He just wasn't getting it. He knew it was just practice. He knew his brother posed no real threat, and yet his body refused to believe it.

"Tell me again how long it took you to get the hang of this?" Matt asked.

"Pfft... I don't know. It's been a while."

"Do you remember when it first happened? The change, I mean."

"I think I was about fifteen. Dad had just started training me a couple of months earlier. I couldn't wait to finally shift. It seemed like the most exciting thing in the world to me. To finally grow up," Jamie said, a wistful smile playing on his lips.

"Oh yeah? I can tell you it freaked me the hell out when it first happened to me."

"That's just because you didn't know."

"Yeah, and it hurt like hell too," Matt added.

"Well, that's there. Those early days were pretty painful."

Jamie handed him another pair of track pants, which Matt accepted with a nod. He put them on and sat down on the floor resting his head in his hands. It just wasn't right. He was in there, being held essentially against his will, and in trying to fight the exact thing he'd been suppressing for all of his adult life, he'd shifted more often in the past forty-eight hours than he had done in years.

And meanwhile, he couldn't get one specific image out of his head.

Leah's expression when she'd seen him in her

bedroom. The sheer terror in her eyes. It hurt, knowing he'd added to her ordeal by bursting in there looking like a big furry monster. He had to fix it somehow. But how could he do that while he was stuck in here?

"Anyway, how long? How long do you think it'll be before I can go back home?" Matt asked.

Jamie frowned at him, his head cocked to one side just like he used to do when they were kids, and Matt said something stupid. Just that look made him want to transform all over again and roar.

"You're not ready."

"Fine, I'm not ready, but you gotta gimme something! I've got responsibilities, and I'm losing my mind here," Matt argued.

"Bullshit, you've got a human girlfriend who is under close watch by Margaret and the rest of the team ever since you recklessly exposed the existence of our entire race to her," Jamie retorted.

"How was I supposed to know what I could and couldn't expose when nobody bloody told me what I was, huh?"

They stared each other down, two grown men who were bickering pretty much like how they used to fifteen years ago. In the end, it was Jamie who backed down.

"Look, I can understand the situation you're in, but you've got to understand that these people-" Jamie gestured at the door of Matt's cell; the main Alliance workspace was just on the other side. "Are scrutinizing your and her every move. If you make contact, you'll both be in trouble. You don't want that, do you?"

Matt sighed. No, he didn't want that at all. But he had to make sure Leah was all right.

"How about you focus on your training," Jamie insisted. "And I'll check in on Margaret every so often to figure out what's happening with your human."

Matt nodded. Okay. That was a fair compromise, for now.

Although he'd been at the base and interacted a bit with members of his own species for days now, it was still weird to hear Jamie talk about humans like they were so different.

Matt, who had grown up around only humans, was, of course, painfully aware of how badly he'd fitted in with them, but he still couldn't consider them the *other*. To him, it was Henry, Margaret, the rest of the team - even Jamie - who still seemed alien.

"And how about this. I've finally received the green light from the Alliance Council to let Mom and Dad know you've been found. They're thrilled, obviously, and can't wait for us all to get together once Blacke signs off on it."

Matt felt his heartbeat speed up. The revelation that his, no, *their* parents were still alive after all these years had been a good one, obviously, but he couldn't shake the worry that meeting him would be more of a disappointment to them than a joyous reunion.

He hadn't exactly grown into the sort of person - bear - they would have wanted him to.

"What's up? you don't look too happy to hear that?" Jamie asked.

"Nah, I am," Matt said, but realized immediately he'd failed to hide the doubt in his tone. "I just don't think I'm all that, if you know what I mean."

"Shit, are you kidding me? You're alive, which is pretty much all they've wanted all these years. And finally, I can show face at home again as well."

Matt had to grin. "Yeah, after over a decade of being the son who lost their other son?"

"Something like that." Jamie shot him a wry smile.

It was a rare thing, to recognize weakness in Jamie. He put on a hard front, but this little glimpse made Matt wonder if perhaps he wasn't the only Brown boy who had grown up a little messed up.

"So. Ready to get back to your training? The sooner you get the hang of this, the sooner we can all get back to our normal lives," Jamie said.

"Sure, just one more thing. Is that why you go by Abbot?"

"I didn't want to have to go through the same story over and over again. In these circles, everyone has heard of the Brown abduction case..."

Matt remembered how weird it was to feel everyone's stares when he'd first been faced with the Alliance team. "Fair enough."

"You know what?" Jamie asked.

"What?"

"You and I just had an entire argument without you sprouting fur or claws. That's not bad at all." Jamie grinned at him, then, without prior warning charged at him, pushing Matt against the wall with a loud thud.

It hurt, and the concrete might as well be covered in ice, but instead of responding with aggression, Matt focused on another image. Another source of calm. The image of Leah balancing an impossible number of little parcels in her arms on the way to her car.

He had to get through this. And if Jamie indeed managed to keep an eye on what Margaret was up to, perhaps it wouldn't turn out so bad.

She was fine; she had to be. Leah was a strong woman, and once he got back home, he'd explain everything to her.

Matt saw the next blow coming from the corner of his eye and ducked out of the way, causing Jamie to hit his fist into the wall.

"Damn," Jamie growled, as he turned around.

A glimmer of something different appeared in his eyes. A fiery amber, which Matt had only seen a few times before: in his own eyes in the mirror, when he'd felt his sanity slipping away.

"Gotcha! How does it feel to be pissed off, bro? Looks like you're very close to losing control yourself now," Matt quipped.

Jamie frowned. "Very funny, just you wait 'til I get you

again, little one."

Matt scoffed. Little one? Matt was at least as tall, if not taller than Jamie was. And they were both built, more so than regular humans.

He stood his ground for the next attack, both his feet planted firmly on the ground. This time, when Jamie hit him, he felt it rattle his bones despite the gloves. He wanted to turn; he wanted to retaliate so badly, but he didn't budge. Only the slightest flutter passed over his skin, its texture changing only for a moment, before morphing back into its usual, human appearance.

"Better. And again," Jamie ordered.

Matt took a deep breath, fighting with every fiber in his body against the survival instinct that had developed in their kind over thousands of years. It's common wisdom in the human world, not to suppress your emotions, and yet that's exactly what this training was about.

How stupid this whole secrecy thing was, anyway. Everyone was afraid of the unknown, so if the objective was not to create fear in humans, wouldn't it actually make sense to be transparent?

None of this would have ever happened if people had just been honest with Matt while growing up. And now he had to pay for it, in this cold, dark, horrible place, with his very own brother trying to rile him up.

Ridiculous.

Matt's jaw tightened as he withstood another one of Jamie's assaults.

"Good job. Keep this up, and we'll be able to progress to the next stage: outdoor training," Jamie remarked.

CHAPTER NINE

For days, Leah had been keeping too much of an eye on the house next door - Matt's house. And yet, she hadn't seen the slightest curtain twitch or sign of movement at all.

It was nerve wracking.

By Thursday, his weekly grocery delivery came and went, and his door didn't open for that either.

That was the last straw for Leah, who had started imagining all sorts of horror scenarios.

What if he hadn't been ignoring her, but something bad had happened to him? What if he was unwell or worse and unable to respond to her repeated messages - or the doorbell? What if more of the same people who had come into her house to take her, had also broken into his place and successfully abducted him before those weird black commando gear people had turned up? But to what end?

It just didn't make sense, and not knowing where Matt was or what he was up to was driving her crazy.

So finally, before the delivery van from the local supermarket had even pulled out of their road, she picked up the phone for one last message.

"If you don't respond, I'm reporting you missing with the police."

She bit her lips and waited, tears stinging in her eyes. How long she should wait for, she wasn't sure, but it was all she could think to do.

When the phone buzzed, about a minute later, she got so startled she almost dropped it to the floor.

"Don't do that. Everything will be explained in time."

From terrified, Leah reverted to being angry. So all this time he had just simply chosen not to answer her! The nerve. And what a weird, impersonal reply as well!

Fine. In that case, she didn't need to concern herself

with this bullshit anymore.

Leah threw the phone onto the counter and started work on the order she should have been focusing on instead of obsessing about Matt.

———•———

Day after day went by, and Leah kept on feeling low. It was like all the joy had been sapped from her, like nothing could make her smile.

And all because of a guy she hadn't even properly met.

It wasn't that she didn't have work to do and just set idle all day. Not at all. She had plenty on her plate. It was just that after a whole day of keeping busy, she had nothing to look forward to anymore. That's what she told herself anyway.

She had never had a large friend circle, only keeping a select few people close. Over the years of working at the call center, with all those night shifts, those few friends had drifted apart as well, so she'd mainly interacted with her colleagues.

In this new place, she had nobody. She certainly wasn't about to count Carrie as a new friend, no matter how often she chose to drop by for a chat - something that had been happening every other day or so since Matt's disappearance.

Leah hadn't told Carrie much about her contact with Matt, only that she'd left him a note to say hello. But for some reason, Carrie must have been suspecting something. That was why she kept coming over, kept prying, however subtly for information about Matt.

It was weird.

Still, the days kept on passing drearily, and Leah started to get used to the emptiness left behind by the uninhabited house next door.

On the tenth night, another strange, windowless van pulled into the street. It was late, so the neighbors would probably be asleep, but not Leah. She was making herself a hot chocolate in the kitchen and happened to be looking out the window when it happened.

The people in black were back.

She took a sip and observed a strange man she'd never seen before get out of the driver's side door and walk to the other side, opening the passenger door for someone else.

Matt.

Leah held her breath.

He was back.

The other man patted Matt on the shoulder, and then they embraced for but a second. The whole scene was eerie.

They seemed so similar. Their hair, their frames, even the way they carried themselves, as though no burden was too heavy to carry, no obstacle too tall to cross.

Her heartbeat sped up against her will.

What did she care if he came back? Matt had been toying with her all along, and especially since that night these people had first shown up.

Leah swallowed the lump that had developed in her throat upon seeing him.

That was when he turned around, and she panicked. Her kitchen was lit up like a stage while the street was much darker. He'd be able to see her much clearer than she could see him.

Shit, shit, shit! She quickly jumped into action and left, pretending to herself that she'd never even noticed any movement outside the window.

He'd assume she hadn't seen him, right?

Way to play it cool, you idiot, Leah chided herself.

After leaving the kitchen, she took a round of her living room and hall, making sure the extra dead bolts she'd had installed were securely locked, and the new alarm system engaged, then hid herself away in her bedroom. Although she wouldn't be able to sleep just yet - especially not now that she knew Matt was back home - there was no need to draw unnecessary attention to herself either.

Leah got into bed and held on to her steaming hot mug with both hands, yet chills kept running down her spine. Why was she so nervous all of a sudden? He was just a guy. Just like all the other guys, who take what they want without for once considering how the other person felt.

Her phone sat beside her, lifeless on the wooden bedside table, practically taunting her. He wouldn't try to get in touch immediately, would he? *Rubbish*! And she wouldn't answer him if he did either.

She put the mug down and brusquely shoved the mobile underneath the pillow beside her.

There was no way, absolutely no way that she would keep on sitting here staring at it, waiting for the buzz of a message. Not now. Not after all that.

———◆———

Morning came, and Leah felt like she'd barely slept, just sort of drifted in and out of a dreamless half-consciousness that hadn't provided much rest.

Matt was still there, after his late night arrival. She didn't know how she knew, but she could feel his presence nearby.

Despite her struggle to get through the night, she did feel somewhat lighter today, after nearly two weeks of having a dark cloud hang over her.

She'd been wondering what if he came back? What if he wanted to get in touch? He hadn't even sent her a single message. Knowing that he wasn't interested, perhaps could give her some closure and enable her to move on. That had to be it. She was feeling a bit better because she could close off that chapter of her life, not at all because he was back home.

It was still quite early, but there wasn't much of a point staying in bed if she couldn't sleep anyway, so Leah got herself up and into the kitchen, ready to start her day. The forecast had foretold clear weather, and she was hoping to finish work early so that she could catch a few rays sitting on her living room sofa before dusk would inevitably set in at around four-thirty in the afternoon. This time of year, the days were depressingly short, so any sunlight was precious.

While waiting for the kettle to boil, a rustling noise came from the front door, like something being pushed through the letterbox. Six o'clock was way too early for the postman, wasn't it?

She wrapped herself up tighter in her oversized knitted cardigan and left the kitchen to investigate. Indeed there it was, a little parcel on her welcome mat.

Leah picked it up and immediately opened the front door to get a glimpse of whoever had delivered it, but the street just looked dark and empty. A gust of cold wind made its way into the house through the open doorway, so she shut it again almost as quickly.

She weighed the packet in her hand. It was small, about the size of two small juice cartons taped together, but much lighter than that.

Should she open it?

Her heart beat a little faster while deciding on her next move. She didn't like the idea of having a random stranger deliver something through her letterbox. What if there was something dangerous inside? Then again, it hardly weighed much, how bad could it be?

She returned to the kitchen and poured herself a cup of tea first. Nothing good can come from a decision made before the first cup of tea, as her dad used to say.

Once ready, she carried both the parcel and the steamy beverage with her into the living room and put both down onto the coffee table.

As cautious as she wanted to be, there was no way curiosity wouldn't get the better of her eventually. She might as well open the thing right away, rather than torture herself any further.

She peeled away the first layer of brown tape with her fingernail, then quickly unraveled the rest. Underneath, a layer of bubble wrap, and then a sealed cardboard box. If the picture on the front was anything to go by, it was a basic mobile phone.

Why would someone send her a phone? And for free, no less.

As she opened the seal and lifted the lid off the small box, a piece of paper fell out the side with a short message scrawled on it.

"Your phone is being monitored. Use this one instead."

Oh damn. It was from Matt, wasn't it?

She wasn't sure what to think. Had he lost his mind completely? What made him think that he could just waltz back into her life after vanishing without explanation for nearly two weeks?

That was it. She was going to give him a piece of her mind, and she might as well use the new phone to do it.

She opened the box fully and switched the gadget on. It only took a minute or so. It didn't have very many apps, or perhaps even a Wifi connection. The phone book had only one number programmed into it, labeled Matt.

Should she call? No, that would be stupid. They'd messaged back and forth plenty, but never actually spoken. Hearing his voice might just make her forget what she wanted to say.

Her moment of indecisiveness didn't last long, because the choice had already been made for her. The phone rang.

Her throat went dry when she saw the caller ID. It was Matt.

CHAPTER TEN

Why wasn't she picking up? It was early, but he knew she was already awake.

Matt put the phone down and scratched his head. They'd had a connection, hadn't they? Before everything went to shit, and he was taken by the Alliance for his so-called training. They'd felt something together; he'd been sure of it at the time, but now doubts were starting to develop.

He'd been away for what, little over a week? Had she dismissed him so quickly?

It made sense, in a way. He wasn't exactly a prize; he knew that.

And to make things worse, at a time when she was already scared to death, he'd climbed into her house full-bear and terrified her even further. Follow that with the Alliance's attempts at managing the situation - and their secret - by convincing her she never actually saw what she thought she saw...

No wonder she'd shut down and wanted nothing to do with him.

Or perhaps she hadn't found the phone yet. That could be the case as well. He'd seen her light on when he dropped the little packet into her letterbox, but perhaps she just hadn't picked it up and opened it yet.

He'd give it a little longer, then try again. It wasn't within him to give up on the situation so quickly, not without ruling out all other possibilities.

Matt took a deep breath and picked up his laptop. So many emails from his clients, their tone ranging from concern to anger right down to dismissal. He ought to write back to them immediately, apologize for his absence, make up some health related reason why he couldn't notify them sooner. Anything would do to salvage his reputation and get his work life back under control.

There was just one problem: none of it seemed important anymore.

He was a bear. Within the blink of an eye, he could turn and rip an attacker to shreds if he wanted to. What the hell was he doing here, typing inane reports about foreign currency fluctuations or what the latest budget would mean to small businesses? None of that stuff mattered.

Leah. She mattered to him.

He had to get in touch with her, explain everything - preferably in a way that the Alliance didn't find out about it - and make things right. Over the course of little over a week, he'd gone from never leaving his house to being stuck at the Alliance base and even heading into a nearby forest to train with Jamie outdoors.

He'd felt the reluctant rays of mid-winter sun on his face. The icy winds cut through his flesh, right to his bones.

He'd emerged from a shell he'd confined himself in for so long; it was unthinkable to just go back to the way things were.

And she - the woman who had given him the benefit of the doubt initially - was right there next door, yet so far away.

He tried her new number again, holding his breath as the phone rang. *Please, pick up!*

Then, rather than the expected recording informing him that the caller cannot be reached, there was a click and a second of static, before he finally heard a voice.

"Hello?" a female spoke softly at the other end.

He wasn't sure what to say. It was like he'd somehow drifted out of reality, and he wasn't actually on the phone with her.

"Leah?" he finally asked.

"That's me."

Oh God. She sounded irritated. Or nervous. Or both. He wasn't sure, not without looking at her.

"I'm so sorry," he blurted out.

"You vanished. No response to any of my messages, except just once, which was just plain odd,"

"I know. And I can explain; not that I'm trying to make excuses for any of this, I'm not..." Matt rested his forehead in his palm. How was he going to make this right?

She didn't respond immediately, just sighed.

"What did you mean they're spying on me?"

"It's a long story. Probably best we don't do this now. Who knows if they're listening in somehow, despite the new phone."

"Okay..." She didn't sound convinced.

How strange. This was the first time they'd spoken on the phone. He couldn't shake the worry that he'd say something to fuck it all up, but still her voice seemed familiar to his ear. Like he knew her way better than was possible after merely talking via Whatsapp for a couple of weeks.

"I know it doesn't seem like it right now, but I really care about you. I just hope you'll give me the chance to make things right," he said.

She sighed again, and the thought that he'd hurt and disappointed her affected him deeply.

"I'm not someone you can toy with. Just know that."

Her words stung even more. Matt closed his eyes and tried to focus, but his emotions were all over the place. He had to do something more than this. Something compelling, that would show her the real him.

"I wouldn't do that. Please believe me."

"If you say so."

While he was away, he'd thought he'd just come back and explain, but this was way harder than he could have imagined. Her resistance was making him realize how fragile relationships could be. How one misstep could unbalance everything and destroy what trust they'd built up between them.

Was there even any hope? He didn't know the first thing about love or women even. He'd been away from it all for too long to know the rules.

He needed to think, to devise a plan to make it up to her. This was too impersonal, too distant.

"May I come over?" he asked. The question surprised him as much as it might have done her.

She didn't answer straight away. Matt wondered what would be worse, if she rejected him, or if she said yes, and he had to follow through on his word.

"Let me be totally honest," she started. Her voice was still soft but also determined. "The reason I answered your call was mainly to tell you that you just can't do stuff like this. You can't just disappear and expect things to be the same when you return. Things are definitely not the same for me."

Matt wasn't sure how to respond. "Just let me explain." He pinched the bridge of his nose to ward off the growing tension in his chest.

He'd trained so hard to get back home, to get this crazy urge to shift under control. He'd been kept locked up in a cold cell, even beaten up by his own brother, but none of that came even close to the amount of stress he was under right now.

He'd enjoyed his conversations with Leah; they'd made him feel normal. Knowing that they'd talk every night had made him feel wanted. The idea of losing all that was too much to bear.

"It's not the same. I understand that," Matt had to force each word to come out calmly when all he wanted to do was scream. "Leah."

"Yes?"

He could hardly hear her response through the haze that overwhelmed his senses, the rush of blood that tried to deafen him. It took all his focus, all of his strength to keep himself from shifting.

"Words can't explain how important you are to me. Allow me to prove it."

The silence between them seemed to last forever.

"Fine. Come over," she said.

Matt breathed a sigh of relief. She was giving him a second chance, even if he realized the battle was far from won.

"Thank you. I don't want to use the front door, just in case someone's watching. Meet me out back?" he asked.

"Whatever you say." With those words, Leah hung up.

Matt stared at his phone, which had gone dark in his hand. This was it. The moment of truth. Had he learned anything from his time with Jamie? Would Leah accept his apology? Would she accept *him*?

It took a moment to force himself into action. How ridiculous. This past week, he'd learned that he could fight. That he was at least four times as strong as a normal human man, but the thought of facing this beautiful, fragile creature next door terrified him. Despite all his strength, she could defeat him with just a look, or a word even. For some reason, she had all the power and he had none.

Still, this was what it meant to be a man, probably. To be faced with something seemingly impossible, and then do it anyway.

It was now or never. If he didn't follow through on this chance to make things right with her, after having to beg for it, she'd never respect him.

He ran his hands through his hair, checking himself in the mirror once to make sure he at least looked somewhat presentable, even if he felt like a failure at the moment.

Matt brushed himself off, put the phone down on the first surface he passed by on the way to the back of the house, and unlocked the French door of the sun room.

In the still dark backyard, he could still see that everything was how he'd left it. The paving stones waiting to be laid for his new barbecue area, the soil needed to top up the flower beds. All these reminders of projects that suddenly didn't seem important anymore.

The heavy wooden table which he'd used that night to climb over the top unseen and unheard still stood next to the fence as well.

Next door, a creaking noise signaled her arrival.

He took a deep breath and jumped onto the table, then cleared the top of the fence in one swift motion, without looking across first. Seeing her beforehand would no doubt throw him off and ruin his entrance.

A split second later, he found himself on the moist lawn he'd landed on just over a week earlier. This time, the object of his affection wasn't inside under threat. Instead, she stood right there in front of him, her arms crossed and gaze averted.

Before he could even say anything to her, so many conflicting emotions filled him, he found it hard to find the right words. These weren't his feelings, not even close.

That's when she looked up at him and allowed their

eyes to meet. No, they weren't his feelings. They were hers.

He wasn't concerned anymore about losing her, or how scared he'd been about explaining things face-to-face. His fears were nothing compared to what she'd felt all the time he'd been gone.

The transformation was over before he had the chance to stop it.

CHAPTER ELEVEN

When Matt had just lept over the fence, Leah didn't really want to look him in the eye. It seemed to intimate and made her feel too vulnerable.

And then suddenly, she didn't have a choice anymore.

There he was: the impossible. No matter how hard her brain tried to tell her that what she'd seen wasn't real, there stood the bear from that night when everything had changed. Seeing the metamorphosis with her own two eyes answered a bunch of questions and inspired a whole host of new ones.

"What the...," Leah mumbled.

The animal which had formerly been Matt looked startled, then immediately changed back into his former self.

Leah wasn't sure whether to believe what she'd just witnessed or take the easy way out of believing everything Margaret had told her. Stress-induced hallucinations seemed like a more plausible explanation than accepting that a person had actually just managed to shift their entire body-structure around to grow into a huge bear, fur, claws and all, and then back again into a human being.

"Shit, I didn't mean for that to happen," Matt stammered, both hands up in the air as he backed away from Leah.

She wasn't sure how to respond. As shocked as she'd been seeing his other form, he was still bloody distracting standing in front of her butt-naked. It took him a moment to realize what had happened and to pick up some of the shredded clothes off the ground between them and hold them up in front of the most pertinent parts of his exposed physique.

"I knew it. I knew that what I'd seen was true. I just didn't know how to explain it," Leah whispered, her eyes now glued on his chiseled chest.

He was a beautiful man. She'd already realized that the first time she'd laid eyes on him through the fence dividing their properties. But there was something else she couldn't look away from. There were scars, bruises, and scratches, which had barely begun healing, all over his skin.

Matt turned away, which revealed that his back was covered in more of the same blemishes.

"What happened to you?" Leah asked, taking a step forward.

He looked in her direction again, and then glanced down at himself.

"Oh, this? It's nothing."

"It doesn't look like nothing." Leah reached out for him, but he retreated instantly, hitting his back against the fence.

"I'm sorry. I don't know what I was thinking, coming over here explaining everything to you. What a great job I'm doing so far," Matt mumbled.

He seemed torn. Like part of him wanted to jump over that fence and run, and yet his feet weren't cooperating.

"Well, you have my attention now," Leah remarked.

Matt looked up, and, for the first time, they both allowed themselves to truly see the other. Their eyes were glued together, with neither in a hurry to look away. It would have been easier to back down, to not let the other see the vulnerabilities written on their faces.

But there didn't seem any more need to pretend.

"I thought you just left," Leah whispered.

"I had no choice," Matt responded.

Leah couldn't be sure how she did, but she could sense that it was true. "I know that now."

"I thought I lost you," Matt seemed to say, but his lips weren't moving.

Still, it was his voice Leah heard in her head. Perhaps now she was finally losing it and hearing things that weren't there. It felt real, though, and she didn't have the energy to question it beyond that.

She'd never been the emotional type, but this past week had done its best to chip away at her defenses. And now, after everything seemed to want to work itself out, she couldn't hold back the tears anymore.

"How is this even possible?" Leah asked, though she wasn't really after an answer just yet.

Don't cry, Matt's eyes seemed to say.

How ridiculous, eyes can't speak. Then again, if some men can turn into bears, perhaps those same men *can* also speak with their eyes.

"I'm not crying," Leah protested, but sounded so miserable, it was actually kind of funny.

"How about we go inside?" Matt suggested, but then looked down at himself and paused. "Perhaps I should wear something first, though. This is far from appropriate."

That was enough to push Leah's buttons, and she started to giggle.

"Oh yeah, it's all fine flashing a girl in her backyard, but you best wear something to come in the house."

Matt glanced up at her again, and then a smile broke through his previously stony expression as well. "Point taken. But it'll only take a second."

With those words, Matt lept over the fence again, leaving Leah behind on her own.

She still couldn't quite believe what had happened. All

of it was so far removed from what any reasonable person would consider possible, that laughing seemed like the most sensible response. He'd seemed genuine when he apologized, when he explained that he had no choice. And as much as she might have tried to fight it, his presence had an inexplicable effect on her. Like they were somehow meant to find a way to work through their issues.

He would explain what had happened these past weeks, and she would listen. That's all. No big deal.

And then...

Leah blushed before she could finish the thought. By that time, Matt was back, fully clothed and much quicker than Leah had expected him to be.

"I'm almost disappointed you found something to wear," she teased.

"Oh it's like that, is it?" Matt grinned at her.

They just looked at each other for a moment. With each passing second, the butterflies in Leah's stomach seemed to multiply, until she could take it no longer.

"Come in. It's freezing out here." She waved him over.

As Matt approached her, she could no longer recall what exactly it was they were meant to do or talk about. All she could focus on was his face, with those brown eyes which seemed to see right into her. His lips, just full enough to soften his otherwise masculine and angular face.

Rather than step aside to let him enter, Leah stood glued in place. How empty she'd felt while he was gone. And although she hadn't even heard his full explanation yet, everything seemed right again.

He stood right in front of her now, with barely a foot between them. It was only now that she realized how much taller he was. He towered over her and made her feel small, which was unusual, but she loved it.

Leah closed her eyes and inhaled. Sweet, with a hint of

pine. Was that his aftershave?

Either way, his scent went straight to her head. She couldn't resist him. She didn't want to.

Leah tip-toed and wrapped her arms around Matt's neck, and although he flinched for a moment, he soon returned the embrace. It was as though she could feel his heartbeat speed up along with her own. And the tension she felt grow inside of her fed off of his excitement too.

I want to kiss you, Leah thought.

She didn't expect a response, but when she opened her eyes again, there he was, leaning down to get closer to her eye level. Their lips finally connected, after the shortest of hesitations which only served to heighten her anticipation.

And then, Leah could feel him. Not just his lips against hers, his breath tickling her face, or his arms cradling her, but feeling his emotions. It seemed as though from the moment they touched, they had started becoming one.

She could see glimpses of what felt like memories coming from him. How he'd watched her move in and how he'd yearned for her ever since. She also saw bits of their time apart, how he'd worked hard to understand his true nature and figure out how to control it. The images didn't come in any particular order, but more like pieces of a giant jigsaw puzzle, which Leah managed to connect somewhat in order to make sense of it all.

Matt pulled away and immediately the stream of information stopped.

"Did you feel that?" he asked.

"Yeah."

"I guess that's how Mom and Dad did it," he mumbled.

"What?"

"Oh. I guess it's another bear thing. I've never known anyone else who could do it. Communicate like that, without words."

"Ah." Leah had so many questions but couldn't quite focus enough to voice any one of them. She just wanted the connection back. To feel Matt as part of her own being again.

Luckily, she didn't need to spell it out for him because he was after exactly the same thing.

"We should probably take this slow," Matt whispered between kisses.

He didn't mean it, though. His mind was filled with images a lot more explicit than mere kisses, which spurred her own imagination into action. Before she got the chance to reply, she found herself floating. Not in a figurative sense, but she was actually up in the air, cradled in Matt's muscular arms.

"Whoa, careful!"

"Don't worry. I'm not going to drop you." His voice was hoarse with desire, giving her oh so delicious goosebumps. And with those last words, he carried her over the threshold of her back door, right into the hall leading to the bedroom.

She didn't care that her bed wasn't made. Okay, she didn't care *much*. It didn't matter that there was a pile of laundry on a chair, making the room look messy.

He certainly didn't seem to notice it as he marched straight to the bed and laid her down gently onto her back.

All Matt had eyes for now was her. If she focused, she could see herself through his eyes.

It was a strange experience and a completely new view for her. Her features seemed softer, more feminine and sensual than when she looked at herself in the mirror. Though it was certainly different, it was unmistakably her.

Could he see what she saw also?

Those eyes, a deep, warm amber so inviting she could scarcely look away.

The only thing more inviting was the promise of tempting flesh now covered by the button-down shirt he had on. She already knew what hid beneath the soft cotton and couldn't wait to discover the same by touch.

"I hope it doesn't hurt?" Leah asked as the first of the bruises she'd spied earlier came into view while unbuttoning his shirt.

"Can't feel a thing," he whispered against her neck.

"You're gorgeous," Leah breathed once she had finished with all the buttons.

"Your turn," Matt spoke in a low growl that made the hairs on the back of her neck stand up. Oh God, how could she resist this man?

He kneeled between her legs, giving her space to raise herself slightly, then he tugged her top off, leaving her barely covered by the rather sensible bra she'd worn this morning. It didn't stay on for long, though, his impatient fingers made sure of that.

Again, her mind was filled with images of herself, filtered by his consciousness. She'd always been confident enough in herself, but never felt as sexy as right now. Neither had she known this lust, this passion growing inside of her that was just begging to be let loose.

I don't want it slow, she thought.

He stared at her, his eyes quite a bit darker than normal.

Your wish is my command.

Leah closed her eyes and lay back onto the bed again while Matt tore off first her jeans and then his own. She was ready. She was his.

CHAPTER TWELVE

It had been a while since the last time Matt had been with a woman. Quite a while actually; the last time he had been no more than a nervous teenager, impatiently fumbling in the dark.

Right now couldn't have been more different.

Leah made everything different.

He'd already known that her presence had made it so much more difficult to control the beast that lurked within him. But he could have never guessed just how hard it was to pace himself now that things had become a lot more intimate between them.

His bear didn't as such want to come out anymore, but he did have very specific wants and desires.

He wanted to possess her completely. To spread her wide and take her. Right now. No compromises.

Matt took a deep breath as he admired Leah's naked flesh in front of him. Flawless skin. Generous curves in all the right places. He ached to touch her all over, but at the same time, it seemed almost criminal to rush things.

There could only be one first time.

One first time for his lips to connect with the soft pink of her nipples.

One first time for him to taste her sweet nectar.

One first time for his cock to enter her.

He wanted to do it all, slowly, so that he would remember it forever.

At the same time, he heard her voice in his mind, spurring him on to take her. How he wanted to give in to her demands, to please her.

He reached down between her legs and gently explored her folds. She was slick with her own juices already, had been for quite some time; he'd been able to pick up on the scent of her arousal from the moment they'd first kissed out in the garden.

She moaned and pressed her hips up, forcing his finger to touch her more deeply. Then, as their eyes locked, something in him snapped.

He could hold back no more.

And so he spread her thighs wide and pushed his swollen cock against her opening. She was tight; perhaps it had been a while for her too.

Either way, it didn't matter. It was clear that this, what they felt together, was beyond anything either of them had experienced with any other partner. No matter what had come before, this was a new beginning; a new life of sorts.

When he entered her, an even louder moan escaped her lips. He felt a red haze descend over him, putting him in a kind of trance. He could feel her pleasure inside of him. He could hear the blood rush through her veins, the feverish pace of her heartbeat.

As he sped up, he could sense exactly how she wanted it: the faster and harder he went, the more intense her reactions were.

How beautiful she looked, her lips slightly parted, eyes full of desire for him. He so needed to hear her scream. To see those beautiful lips opened wider and gasping for air.

So he made it happen. Harder. Deeper.

His cock started to tingle and pulsate. He was getting close himself, which in turn seemed to spur her on.

Their climax came so quickly it almost snuck up on him. Leah hit the point of no return first, twitching, quivering underneath him as she screamed out his name.

He wasn't sure what happened next, only that he found

himself drowning in waves of bliss as he filled her with his hot seed.

Although he'd always been fit, it took a while for him to catch his breath.

"That was..."

"Yeah," she gasped.

"I love you," he whispered.

She pressed her lips together and stared at him with those big, dark eyes of hers. *I love you too*, he could hear her say in his mind.

He wasn't sure how he knew, but he was certain that now they had truly become one. Their bond would not be broken, not by time, distance or interference by other people.

This was it. They were a couple.

———————◆———————

Matt wasn't sure when exactly he'd fallen asleep. It was unusual for him to fall asleep so easily, more so because it was the middle of the day. He hadn't slept at daytime since his childhood.

He looked over at Leah, who still snoozed beside him. Her dark locks were spread out over the pillow, but he could still make out how tousled they'd become during their passionate romp earlier. Watching her made him smile.

Despite being in this bed for the very first time, he felt at home. And it was all because she was here.

It hadn't been easy, getting to this point together. A lot had tried to stand in their way.

Matt thought about what brought them here. The glances stolen at each other through windows or fences. The messages back and forth that had sparked an initial friendship, which inevitably wanted to develop into something more.

He remembered their conversations, including the very first time she'd overtly started to flirt with him. He'd been an idiot, holding back, trying to deny his feelings in the hopes that simply talking to her would be enough. Fate, as well as Leah, of course, had had other ideas.

Flowers *and* chocolates, she'd said she wanted. He hadn't given her either so far. That had to change.

Now that they were together, he would give her whatever she'd want. He'd give her the world if he could.

Finally, Leah stirred, opening her eyes and blinking a few times as they adjusted against the bright daylight in her bedroom. In their hunger for each other, they'd never even closed the curtains.

"I fell asleep," Leah remarked.

"Me too." Matt smiled at her.

"I feel so... lazy." Leah stretched her arms but made no attempt to get up.

Recalling his earlier thoughts, Matt realized that although he still didn't have either chocolates or flowers to give her, the very least he could do was provide some caffeine.

"How about I make us a cup of tea?" he suggested.

"That would be lovely."

Matt leaned over and kissed her lips. So sweet. In all the frenzy earlier, he hadn't even stopped to notice her fragrance. Like vanilla and spring blossoms.

Then he got up and made his way to the kitchen. Although he'd only been in her house briefly once before, he could find his way blindfolded if he had to. Their bungalows shared the same layout, the only difference being the sunroom he'd added to the back of his house years ago.

He put on the kettle and out of habit scanned the street

outside. It was quiet, save for one black van parked right in front of the house.

Shit. Had the Alliance found out about them?

Matt turned the kettle off and rushed back through the lounge towards the hall, then stopped dead in his tracks when he saw a very familiar figure.

"Henry." Matt turned to face him and folded his arms. His body squarely blocked the hallway leading to the rest of the house and with it, Leah. No matter what, these people wouldn't take Leah. No way. He wouldn't let it happen.

"Matt. You know why they sent me here?" Henry asked in a low voice.

"I can guess, and before you say anything else, no, you can't take her."

Henry sighed. "There's been a lot of enemy activity in the city, and everyone is on high alert."

"I don't care. I'm not going to let you take her." Matt felt his muscles tighten, his skin crawl. He was ready to shift and charge if the situation demanded it.

"Relax, I'm not going to take her." Henry ran his hand through his hair and started pacing around the room. "The truth is, I'm not happy with the status-quo. What happened to you, here, it's not right. None of this is right."

"Okay... What are you trying to say, exactly?"

"I have a plan to make things right, but it's going to take some time to set up."

"Shoot."

"Firstly, this is for you." Henry retrieved something from his pocket and handed it to Matt. An SD card, like the ones you put into a digital camera.

"You might want to keep that safe. I caught her red-handed taking pictures, so she wouldn't have had time to make another copy."

Matt weighed the little card in his hand, then looked up again. "You caught who? Taking pictures of what exactly?"

Henry cocked his head to the side. "Your neighbor, Caroline. I'm sure you can guess what she was taking pictures of without me spelling it out."

Matt swallowed. Carrie? He'd known she was a gossip, but to actually spy on the two of them? He would have never expected her to go that far.

"You seem confused. See, we finally managed to crack one of the guys who was at this house that night. One of the Sons of Domnall."

"Right..."

"He mentioned a female collaborator who had tipped them off."

No way. Carrie had sent those people here to attack Leah? And for what, to try to draw *him* out?

"That doesn't make any sense. Carrie and I grew up together. If the people who took me knew what I was, and Carrie is involved with them too, why would she send those guys after me now?"

"Who knows what these people were thinking. If one faction even talks to the other. Before you burst into the house fully shifted, these people weren't even sure you were one of ours." Henry shrugged.

"Anyway, so what do you want in return for this?" Matt nodded down at the card in his hand.

"It's not like that. I don't want anything in return. I want you to consider my idea carefully, and if you agree, only then do I want your help when the time is right."

"Tell me."

"I-" Henry took a deep breath. "I want to go public."

Matt raised an eyebrow.

"Think about it. None of this would have ever happened if people knew about our kind."

"What about the whole secrecy thing Jamie was telling me about?"

"Oh, the Alliance will fight us every step of the way. That's why we've got to be careful until all the pieces are in place."

Matt scratched his chin. Was it a trap? Was Henry just probing him to see where his loyalties lie? But that didn't seem like the guy; he'd always seemed quite straightforward. An honest man. Margaret, now *her* he could imagine to do something underhanded like this, but not Henry.

"What do you need?" Matt asked, finally.

"People. Good, loyal people who believe that openness is the way forward."

"I can't help you with that. I don't even know anyone."

"That's okay. I just want to know if I can call on you when the time comes." Henry looked Matt in the eye as he waited for an answer.

Matt considered the idea and considered the man standing before him. Ever since he found out about his true nature, he'd questioned the same things, wondered if things wouldn't have turned out better if he had known about his true nature sooner.

And Henry... the frustration he had shown earlier about what he had been sent in to do here seemed genuine. Matt took a deep breath and decided to take a chance.

"Okay. I'm in," Matt said.

Henry exhaled, as if he'd been holding his breath the whole time while waiting for Matt's response.

"Right, well, that's good news. Just so you know, you won't have to worry about your neighbor snooping around anymore. I've got her in the back of the van already."

"Great," Matt said, though he still couldn't quite believe Carrie's involvement in all of this.

"I'm going to head back now and tell everyone I found no evidence of you and the human woman being involved with one-another. You take care now."

"Okay, thanks," Matt mumbled, and watched Henry turn around and march out of the lounge, through the adjoining entrance hall and out the front door.

What a bizarre conversation.

Outside, an engine purred to life, and a vehicle - the van, most likely - pulled away and drove off.

"Who were you talking to?" Leah asked, resting her hand on Matt's shoulder. He hadn't even heard her walk up behind him.

"That's a long, weird story." Matt turned, and put his arms around Leah's waist.

She smiled at him and tiptoed to give him a peck on the lips. With her around, it was easy to think that everything was just going to work itself out.

"I'm not going anywhere. Now how about we have that cup of tea, and you tell me everything," she suggested.

He smiled back at her. "All right."

She took his hand, and they walked back into the kitchen together. A quick glance out the window revealed that all was quiet. As if Henry had never even come by.

EPILOGUE

It had been a long five-hour drive to Applecross Bay, filled with awkward silences. Leah was glad that Jamie, Matt's eerily similar looking brother, was driving. Not only did it give her the chance to admire the pretty scenery on the way, she wasn't even sure her little car would have made it this far.

Matt, who sat in the front seat next to Jamie, wasn't quite as receptive to the views; he had other things on his mind. Leah had been able to sense his concerns, obviously.

At last, they pulled into a gravel driveway leading to a solitary house nestled among the sand dunes surrounding the coastline. So this was where the two brothers were born.

"You ready?" Jamie turned the key to switch off the ignition and then turned to face Matt.

Matt didn't answer straightaway.

Leah squeezed his shoulder. *It'll be fine. They're your parents. They'll be thrilled to have you back.*

I know, but... Ah, screw it.

"Sure. Let's go," Matt said.

One by one they undid their seat belts and got out of the car. Jamie led the way up the gravel path leading to the porch, and Matt followed reluctantly. It was strange how similar the two brothers looked, and yet how different their personalities were.

Jamie was so serious, almost cold in everything he did, while Matt was a lot more sensitive and warm. Perhaps it only felt that way because Leah didn't know Jamie all that well. Or more likely, because she could tell he thought it unwise for her to be here with Matt. She was an outsider, after all, no matter how hard Matt tried to convince her otherwise.

Either way, Jamie's disapproval hadn't dissuaded her. Matt had been worrying about this family reunion for a while now, and she was set on being here for emotional support if nothing else.

As they climbed the steps, the net curtain beside the front door moved, and almost immediately after, someone opened the door.

"I don't believe it! You're really here!" a female voice said.

The elderly woman who appeared in the doorway was obviously Matt and Jamie's mother. The similarities between the three of them were striking, but it was Matt who had taken after her the most.

"Your father is inside. He's not been keeping too well, I'm afraid," Matt's mother said. "I still can't... When we last saw you, you were so little. We thought you were gone forever." Her voice cracked with emotion.

Matt seemed lost for words, and even Jamie didn't have anything to add. Not that that mattered to their mom, who couldn't stop talking.

"Anyway, I've made your favorite. At least, it used to be your favorite when you were little. You do still like Apple Pie, don't you?" she asked.

Matt nodded. "Thanks, Mom."

"Oh, you sweet boy." She reached out and put her arms around Matt. "Why don't we go inside and say hello to your father. And who's this?"

Suddenly Leah found herself in the foreground. Matt's mother stepped up to her and smiled. "Forgive the boys their manners; they've forgotten to introduce you!"

"Leah," Leah said while offering her hand. "Matt's..."

she wasn't sure how to finish that statement. Girlfriend sounded awfully juvenile.

"My fiancée," Matt chimed in and put his arm around Leah's shoulder.

Although they'd been inseparable ever since his return from the Alliance, they hadn't formally discussed the future yet. Hearing him introduce her as his fiancée made Leah's heart skip a few beats.

"Oh! How lovely to meet you," Matt's mom said. "What wonderful news, congratulations, you two! We've not just got our youngest son back, but a daughter as well. Jamie, you should take a leaf out of your brother's book and settle down as well. You're not getting any younger."

Jamie sighed. "Yes, Mom."

Leah couldn't suppress a smile. For someone as stoic and in control as Jamie seemed, it was hilarious to see this family dynamic.

Now that the introductions were over, they all moved indoors, Matt and Jamie's mother leading the way. The interior of the house looked like a time capsule left over from the 1970s. A lot of earthy tones and old-fashioned floral drapes. They probably hadn't changed a thing in years.

Leah glanced over at Matt, who silently took it all in. He seemed to recognize bits of the house and watching him as he made his way through his childhood home made her a bit emotional as well.

"David, look who's here," Matt's mom said as they entered the lounge.

Matt's dad, who had been watching TV up to this point looked up and cracked a smile which seemed to wrinkle up his entire face.

"My boys. Together at last. Don't mind if I don't get up. The old leg's been giving me a bit of trouble lately."

"Dad," Matt whispered and walked up to the armchair.

The old man reached out for him, and they embraced awkwardly.

"And look, Matt brought his fiancée, Leah, as well." Matt's mom beamed.

"Ah, I see." Matt's dad smiled at Leah. It was awkward suddenly being the center of attention. "Welcome to the family, lass."

Leah smiled and shook his hand. "Sit down, everyone," Matt's mom said "I hope you're a tea drinker, Leah? I haven't catered for coffee."

"Oh yes, tea would be lovely."

Matt and Leah sat down on the sofa, while Matt's mom left the room, only to reappear shortly after carrying a tray full of cups, saucers and a teapot. Jamie sat further away, pulling up a dining chair for himself.

It was only natural that Matt felt awkward in the company of his folks. After all, they'd been separated for so long. They all waited in silence while Matt's mom distributed the cups and poured the tea.

Once everyone had a cup in their hand, and conversation slowly did get underway, suddenly it was Jamie who looked most out of place.

"Pie?" Matt's mom offered, and Leah gladly accepted a plate.

"Do tell us what you've been up to all these years? How have things been for you?" she asked Matt.

He answered diplomatically, leaving out the difficulties he'd faced in his adult life and focused on his teen years instead.

"How about work, son? What do you do for work?" his dad asked.

"I write, mostly articles and reports about financial matters."

"Oh, a writer! That's wonderful," his mom chimed in.

The more they talked, the more comfortable the atmosphere became.

"And what about you two, have you set a date yet?" his mom asked, her eyes wide with anticipation.

Leah glanced at Matt and found that he was already looking at her.

Have we? Leah thought.

You tell me, Matt replied.

Tomorrow if you're ready. Leah smiled as Matt took her hand.

"Not yet, perhaps we can come up with something together. It would be no good unless you're both there as well," Matt responded to his mom.

"But of course, we'll be there. Wouldn't miss it for the world," Matt's dad said.

"First, though, what are you all doing for Christmas? Wouldn't it be lovely to finally have a proper family Christmas again? Unless you're going to celebrate with your parents, Leah?" Matt's mother asked.

Leah shook her head. "No plans yet. My Dad passed eight years ago."

"Oh, I'm so sorry to hear that. What about your mother?"

Leah shrugged. "She died when I was very young. It had been just Dad and me for as long as I can remember."

Matt squeezed her hand gently. Even though it had been years since the loss of her dad, talking about it still hurt.

"Ah," his mom said. "Well, it's been decided then. You must come up for Christmas. What do you think, Jamie?"

Jamie, who had been sitting silently in the corner, cleared his throat. "Umm, actually I have to work over the holidays. Sorry about that."

Weird. The Alliance were a strange bunch from what Leah had heard, but to work over Christmas was still a bit extreme. Was it just an excuse on his part?

"Oh, that's too bad." His mom's voice was loaded with disappointment.

"We'll definitely be there, though," Matt said.

"All right then." She smiled. "I'll do a roast like we used to have when you were little."

After this little hiccup, the conversation picked up again, leaving the previous awkwardness behind. Clearly the return of their lost son wasn't enough to repair whatever damage had been done to this family, but it was a start. There obviously was still a lot of love in this house, mixed in with old pain and regret.

The visit lasted for the better part of the afternoon, with everyone - except maybe Jamie - wishing for it not to be cut short. But the Alliance never waited, and he had to be back in Edinburgh early the next day, so they had to make a move.

Their goodbye was bittersweet, with Matt's mom getting emotional again. But at least everyone knew they'd be reunited again soon, for Christmas.

***

ABOUT THE AUTHOR

Dear Reader,

Thanks for reading Scottish Werebear: A New Beginning, Book 4 in the Scottish Werebears Series. Although this is my first published paranormal romance series, I'm not new to writing in general. In fact, my mom still tells me to this day about how I would make up stories, and attempt to record them in my clumsy, shaky handwriting from the moment I learned to read and write. From there I went on to write fan fiction and other stuff meant for my own eyes only.

I've always enjoyed stories of the paranormal. Vampires, shape shifters, witches and magic, all featured in the books I loved the most, even when I was still growing up. But it wasn't until much later that I got into romance. One of the first writers (a self-published author just like me!) I came across was Tina Folsom, via her Scanguards Vampire series. I was hooked. From there I went on to read more paranormal romance until I found a new favorite kind of hero: bear shifters, like the kind written by Milly Taiden, Zoe Chant, and T.S. Joyce. What I love about bears is how they can be all strong and independent, a bit reclusive, and almost grumpy, but they always end up having a heart of gold (plus they tend to know their food, and we all know that a man who can cook is doubly sexy). All that (except for the shifting into a powerful bear) almost exactly describes the sort of man I ended up falling for and marrying in real life, so it's no surprise that this is what I started my publishing career with.

To find out more, check:
LoreleiMoone.com (And why not sign up for the newsletter to be the first to find out about new releases.)

You can also get in touch with me via Facebook (search for Lorelei Moone), or email at info@loreleimoone.com

I also write contemporary romance as L. Moone. If that's something you're interested in, you can take a look at LMoone.com.

x Lorelei